IRON MAIDEN

IN THE STUDIO

IRON MAIDEN

IN THE STUDIO

THE STORIES BEHIND EVERY ALBUM

JAKE BROWN

JB
JOHN BLAKE

Published by John Blake Publishing Ltd,
3 Bramber Court, 2 Bramber Road,
London W14 9PB, England

www.johnblakepublishing.co.uk

www.facebook.com/Johnblakepub facebook
twitter.com/johnblakepub twitter

First published in hardback in 2011

ISBN: 9781843583486

British Library Cataloguing-in-Publication Data:

A catalogue record for this book is available from the British Library.

Design by www.envydesign.co.uk
Printed in Great Britain by CPI Mackays, Chatham, ME5 8TD

1 3 5 7 9 10 8 6 4 2

Papers used by John Blake Publishing are natural, recyclable products made from wood grown in sustainable forests. The manufacturing processes conform to the environmental regulations of the country of origin.

This book is dedicated to several devoted Maiden fans and friends of mine who have reminded me over the years, in one form or another, why this band has always been so bad ass:

Helen Watts for being the truest femme-Metal Maidenhead I know, Richard Kendrick for being the biggest dude-Metal Maidenhead I know, and my cousin B.J. Thieme for giving me my first Iron Maiden tape back in the 1980s!

CONTENTS

ACKNOWLEDGEMENTS

Project thanks: First and foremost I would like to thank my UK publisher John Blake for continuing to support my *In the Studio* series with such cool bands (AC/DC, Motorhead, etc.). Thanks to the following invaluable research sources: Maidenfans.com; Maiden-World.com; CDuniverse.com; Ironmaiden.com; official biographer Mick Wall; all the credited critics whose positive reviews of Maiden's catalogue help to give a more rounded appreciation to newer fans of the band; and, finally, anyone and everyone who might have had a hand in sources for this book.

Personal thank you(s): First and foremost, as always, I would like to thank my parents, James and Christina Thieme-Brown, for continuing to tirelessly support my various artistic goings-on (both literary and musical); my brother Joshua T. Brown (K-9 Catalyst, proud of you, bud); the extended Brown and Thieme families; Alex Schuchard and Jackson Schuchard for being the coolest godson in the world! Thank you, also, to my girlfriend Dena for coming into my life when you did and continuing to make it better and brighter every day since…

Thanks, too, to Andrew and Sarah McDermott; 'The' Sean and Amy Fillinich; Adam Perri; Chris 'See' Ellauri; Matt, Eileen and Kamelya Ellen Peitz; Richard (thanks for the past ten years re Versailles), Lisa and Regan Kendrick; Paul and Helen Watts; Bob O'Brien and Cayenne Engel; Lexi 'Clown' Federov; Rose Reiter and Gerry Plant; MVD Distribution/Big Daddy Music; Aaron 'Whippit' Harmon for continuing to have my back musically week in and out; Joe Viers/Sonic Lounge Studios for ten years of great ears; Andrew McNeice at Melodic Rock; Keavin Wiggins at Antimusic.com; Cheryl Hoahing at *Metal Edge*; Tim at *Brave Words/Bloody Knuckles*; *Rock and Roll Report*; John Lavallo and Take Out Marketing; Bookmasters; Larry, Joel, James and everyone at Arbor Books; Aaron, Gabriel, Victor, John and everyone at SCB Distribution/Rock N Roll Books.

To Jasmin St Claire, thanks for hanging in there – we finally made it! Lemmy Kilmister; Curt and Cris Kirkwood/Dennis; Ben Ohmart/BearManor Media; Jack, Crissy, David, Simon and all at ECW Press; Tony (congrats on beating the big C!) and Yvonne Rose at Amber Books; Richard Anderson at Cherry Red Books; Jason Rothberg and Tracii Guns, thanks for the opportunity to be involved with telling this amazing story; Stephan Jenkins and Third Eye Blind for the opportunity to work on an *In the Studio* book with you! Finally, and without arrogance of any sort, thank you to the music fans who buy and read my books, specifically this series, as you keep them coming. ☺!!!

I have drawn on many different sources in putting together this book and I would particularly like to acknowledge and thank the following:

Iron Maiden – Run to the Hills (third edition), Mick Wall

VH1 Classic Albums Number of the Beast DVD

The Maidenfans.com interview archive. Band-member quotes were sourced from the following interviews (some don't indicate specific print magazine, just the interviewer, date, etc.):

30 June 1982 – Steve Harris interview with journalist Shelly Harris

31 July 1983 – Steve Harris interview with journalist John Styx

31 July 1983 – *Artist* magazine interview with Bruce Dickinson, Steve Harris, Adrian Smith and Dave Murray

30 September 1987 – Unknown source, interview with Steve Harris, Bruce Dickinson, Dave Murray (referenced Maidenfans.com as source)

1 November 1988 – Bruce Dickinson interview with *Kerrang!* magazine

1 January 1990 – Bruce Dickinson interview with *Sports Illustrated*

30 April 30 1992 – Steve Harris and Dave Murray interview with *Raw* magazine

31 May 1992 – Steve Harris interview with *Kerrang!* magazine

30 April 1993 – Bruce Dickinson, Steve Harris and Nicko McBrain interview with *Kerrang!* magazine

31 May 1995 – Blaze Bayley and Steve Harris interview (source unknown, credited to Maidenfans.com)

31 July 1995 – Blaze Bayley interview (source again unknown, credited to Maidenfans.com)

1 October 1995 – Steve Harris and Blaze Bayley interview (ditto)

1 February 1996 – Blaze Bayley interview with journalist Sumit Chandra

1 February 1996 – Blaze Bayley interview with journalist Ram Samudrala

1 February 1996 – Dave Murray interview (source again unknown, credited to Maidenfans.com)

31 August 1996 – Steve Harris interview with Lars Ulrich

31 March 1998 – Janick Gers and Dave Murray interview with *Terrorizer*

31 March 1998 – Blaze Bayley and Steve Harris interview with *Metal Hammer*

31 March 1998 – Blaze Bayley and Steve Harris interview with *Kerrang!*

31 March 1998 – Blaze Bayley interview with *FHM* magazine

30 April 1998 – Dave Murray interview with *Metal Hammer*

30 April 1998 – Blaze Bayley interview with *Vox*

30 April 1998 – Blaze Bayley interview with *Kerrang!*

30 April 1998 – Blaze Bayley and Steve Harris interview with *hockwaves*

30 June 1998 – Steve Harris interview with Sumit Chandra

30 June 1998 – Blaze Bayley interview with *Format Power*

30 June 1998 – Blaze Bayley interview with journalist Sumit Chandra

1 October 1998 – Bruce Dickinson interview with *Rock Brigade*

1 November 1998 – Blaze Bayley and Steve Harris interview with *Metal Hammer*

1 January 1999 – Blaze Bayley interview with Metal-Rules.com

1 February 1999 – Iron Maiden group interview with IronMaiden.com

1 February 1999 – Iron Maiden group interview 2 with IronMaiden.com

1 February 1999 – Dave Murray and Bruce Dickinson interview with *Rolling Stone*

1 February 1999 – Bruce Dickinson interview with Triple JJJ FM Radio

1 March 1999 – Bruce Dickinson and Janick Gers interview with Triple JJJ FM Radio

ACKNOWLEDGEMENTS

31 March 1999 – Adrian Smith interview with unknown source (credited to Maidenfans.com)

1 May 1999 – Bruce Dickinson and Steve Harris interview with journalist Don Kaye

30 June 1999 – Janick Gers interview from the Janick Gers Tour Report

30 June 1999 – Steve Harris and Dave Murray interview with source unknown (credited to Maidenfans.com)

31 July 1999 – Janick Gers and Bruce Dickinson interview with Promethean Crusade

31 July 1999 – Janick Gers interview with Metal-Rules.com

1 August 1999– Bruce Dickinson interview with *Rock Brigade*

30 September 1999– Dave Murray interview with journalist Gary Games

1 December 1999 – Steve Harris interview with journalist Johnny B

1 March 2000 – Nicko McBrain interview with Metal-Sludge.com

1 March 2000 – Bruce Dickinson interview with Promethean Crusade

1 March 2000 – Bruce Dickinson interview with journalist Clay Marshall

1 March 2000 – Bruce Dickinson interview with Intoxicated e–zine

31 March 2000 – Bruce Dickinson interview with journalist Robert Jock

31 March 2000 – Bruce Dickinson interview with The Disseminated Group

30 April 2000 – Steve Harris interview with journalist Johnny B

30 April 2000 – Bruce Dickinson interview with journalist Vinnie Apicella

30 April 2000 – Bruce Dickinson interview with MTV

30 April 2000 – Bruce Dickinson interview with *Classic Rock*

1 June 2000 – Bruce Dickinson interview with journalist Bryan Reeseman

1 July 2000 – Steve Harris interview with Metal-Rules.com

31 July 2000 – Adrian Smith interview with IronMaiden.com FAQs

31 August 2000 – Steve Harris interview with IronMaiden.com FAQs

31 August 2000 – Janick Gers interview with IronMaiden.com FAQs

31 August 2000 – Dave Murray interview with IronMaiden.com FAQs
30 September 2000 – Bruce Dickinson interview with IronMaiden.com FAQs
30 September 2000 – Nicko McBrain interview with IronMaiden.com FAQs
31 August 2001 – Bruce Dickinson interview with Swedish TV station
1 February 2002 – Bruce Dickinson interview with KNAC.com
February 2002 – Bruce Dickinson interview with journalist Fredrik Hjelm
1 March 2002 – Bruce Dickinson and Janick Gers interview with Niclas Müller-Hansen
March 1, 2002 – Bruce Dickinson interview with *Metro*
30 April 2003 – Bruce Dickinson interview with BBC 6Music
31 May 2003 – Nicko McBrain web interview (credited to Maidenfans.com)
30 June 2003 – Bruce Dickinson interview with Asbury Park Press
31 July 2003 – Nicko McBrain interview with Metalfan.nl
31 August 2003 – Iron Maiden group interview with Rock On
31 August 2003 – Janick Gers interview Metal-Rules.com
30 September 2003– Dave Murray interview with *Undercover*
1 November 2003 – Nicko McBrain interview with journalist Svenska Dagbladet
1 December 2003 – Nicko McBrain interview with Metal Masters
1 January 2004 – Dave Murray interview with Bravewords.com
1 September 2004 – Dave Murray interview with journalist Tim Cashmere
1 December 2004 – Steve Harris interview with *Rock Brigade*
1 June 2005 – Bruce Dickinson interview with BBC Live
August 2006 – Bruce Dickinson interview with *Ultimate Guitar*

ACKNOWLEDGEMENTS

September 2006 – Dave Murray interview with *Guitarist*

11 October 2006 – Steve Harris interview with journalist Kevin Purcell

26 October 2006 – Dave Murray interview with LiveDaily.com

Autumn 2006 – Bruce Dickinson interview with *Kerrang!*

8 July 2010 – Iron Maiden interview with *The Aquarian Weekly*

11 July 2010 – Janick Gers interview with Blabbermouth.net

August 2010 – Iron Maiden band interview with Music Radar

August 2010 – Janick Gers interview with Metal-Rules.com

August 2010 – Bruce Dickinson interview with *Kerrang!*

Autumn 2010 – Producer Kevin Shirley Web Blog, www.cavemanproductions.com

August, 2010 – Iron Maiden band interview with *Billboard*

INTRODUCTION

IRON MAIDEN IN THE STUDIO

It could be argued that Iron Maiden is heavy metal's most successful indie band. *Billboard* magazine has pointed out that, in the eyes of the industry at large, Iron Maiden 'has always been an underground attraction'. Other pioneering peers like Motorhead and Metallica have been around for just as long or longer, innovating metal and advancing it commercially to a mainstream level but it was Iron Maiden who began the crossover. As heavy metal went from being just a sub-division of rock to its own signature brand, the BBC acknowledged them as 'pioneers of a new wave of British heavy metal'.

What makes the band's journey to over 100 million albums sold worldwide since forming in 1975 ('with almost no radio or television support', as the BBC added) so enduring? According to co-founding guitarist Dave Murray, the band has lasted these many decades thanks to its group philosophy.

'When we do an album, we put a hundred and fifty per cent into it so, when you listen to an album a few years back and think, "Oh yeah, that sounds good," you know you must've been doing the right thing at that time... We're proud of everything we've done.'

So, too, are their legions of fans around the globe, whose continued championing of the band has earned Iron Maiden, among other honours: the *Kerrang!* Hall of Fame (2005); the BBC's Greatest Metal Band Of All Time award; *Metal Hammer*'s 2009 Golden Gods award; a ranking in the Top 25 on VH1's 100 Greatest Artists of Hard Rock; and the No. 4 spot on MTV's Top 10 Greatest Heavy Metal Bands Of All Time. *Billboard* recently declared that 'Iron Maiden were and are one of the most influential bands of the heavy metal genre,' and MTV.com added that the band have remained 'consistently popular throughout their career'. The band's impressive catalogue now stretches to 15 studio albums spread over 20 years.

MTV.com also noted that Maiden's 'often-imitated' brand of metal would produce some of the 'greatest rock recordings of all time', while *Rolling Stone* observed that Iron Maiden 'distinguished itself from its peers with unusually literate songs ... full of hellish imagery (the melting faces in 'Children of the Damned'), with themes borrowed from films ('The Number of the Beast', inspired by *The Omen II*) and ancient mythology ('Flight of Icarus').

In the pages of *Iron Maiden: in the Studio*, the writing and recording of this catalogue of classics – including such iconic hits as 'The Number of the Beast', 'Flight of Icarus', 'Two

Minutes to Midnight', 'Wasted Years', 'Can I Play with Madness', 'Infinite Dreams', 'Man on the Edge', 'Bring Your Daughter... to the Slaughter', 'The Wicker Man', 'The Trooper', 'Run to the Hills', 'Powerslave' and 'Hallowed Be Thy Name' – are explored in depth for the first time ever.

CHAPTER ONE

IRON MAIDEN (1980)

'There may be no better place to hear how both punk and prog rock informed the New Wave of British Heavy Metal than Iron Maiden's self-titled debut' *Billboard*

'This debut stands as a virtual heavy-metal textbook for anyone eager to learn' iTunes

From day one, bassist/founder Steve Harris has been the driving force behind Iron Maiden. According to *Kerrang*! Harris's edict heading into the band's first album was to make a plan and stick to it. 'That's the key to success. It's a credo that [he] has followed since he started the band on Christmas Day, 1975.' Former lead singer Paul Mario Day – who fronted the band in 1975–76 – later told Maidenfans.com that, even in the early days, 'Steve generally came up with the ideas. I pushed to do more covers but Steve always wanted to stick to his guns and write original stuff. He was amazing like that really and he deserves all the success that he's got.'

In describing some of the band's earliest recordings, Steve Harris told Maidenfans.com years later, 'I've got audio tapes that go right back from 1976, not right from the first gigs, but from the days when we used to play places like the Bridge House. They're a bit dodgy. There's a version of "Purgatory", which was then called "Floating", and it had an arrangement that was a bit different. I've also got a tape of my very first band, Gypsy's Kiss, of us at the Cart and Horses. It might have been the first gig we did. There's a song called "Endless Pit", which later became "Innocent Exile". The tapes exist but I never play 'em to anyone!'

As *Rolling Stone* noted, 'the first incarnation of the band was inspired by the do-it-yourself punk ethos.' But by 1977, according to the *LA Times*, 'while most wannabe London rockers were embracing punk's stripped-down sound and fashionista aesthetic, [Harris was] defiantly creating ... a hairy, denim-clad band that proudly performed heroic, escapist heavy metal.'

In 1979, following numerous line-up changes, the group released an EP, *The Soundhouse Tapes*, on its own label, Rock Hard Records. As guitarist Dave Murray recalled years later to *Metal Hammer*, 'The first Iron Maiden thing we did where I can remember that we were all travelling together was when we went out of London to record what became *The Soundhouse Tapes*, at the Spaceward Studios in Cambridge on New Year's Eve, 1978. There must've been three feet of snow everywhere and we were freezing our balls off, all cramped together in the back of a van.'

Their dedication would pay off. The band recorded the original version of 'Prowler', which, as Harris recalled to journalist John Stix, was a 'very special' song for them. 'When we made *The Soundhouse Tapes*, we took the actual tape to Neal Kay, who was a DJ in north London. He used to have a heavy-metal chart, which was compiled from record requests and printed in the music magazine *Sounds*. "Prowler" got to be No. 1 just from the requests for the demo tape. That's why we had the tape made into a record because so many kids were asking us how they could get hold of the demo tapes ... It was brilliant because that got us work elsewhere as well.'

The bassist added his memory of feeling that there was a certain amount of irony in the fact that *The Soundhouse Tapes* was the very first thing that Iron Maiden had recorded. '[The song] was just a demo ... It really wasn't great quality.'

Still, the quality was good enough for it to sell 5,000 copies within a month of release and land the band a spot on the compilation LP *Metal for Muthas*. This featured early versions of 'Sanctuary' and 'Wrathchild', eventually earning the band a record deal with EMI in late 1979. As the decade turned into 1980, the band made plans to record that spring with producer Will Malone, who had previously worked with Black Sabbath and Meat Loaf, and whose CV would go on to include Peter Gabriel, Simple Minds, Depeche Mode, Seal, The Verve, Dido, Jewel, Oasis and Jeff Beck.

But before Maiden could head into the studio they had to deal with yet another change in their perpetually evolving line-up, following the departure of lead guitarist Paul Cairns.

Years later his replacement, Dennis Stratton of Remus Down Boulevard, recalled to *Praying Mantis* webzine the circumstances that led to him being hired. 'My wife at the time noticed an advert in the *Melody Maker* – "Iron Maiden, EMI recording artists seek guitarist/backing vocalist" – and we were debating whether to write off or phone up for it. I was doing a painting job at Stratford and I got on a bus at Stratford Broadway to go to Canning Town where I was living. A girl came up to me on the bus and said, "You're Dennis Stratton?" I went, "Yeah," and she said, "Oh hello, my name's Lorraine. I'm Steve Harris's girlfriend." And I said, "Yeah?" rather blankly. And she went, "I take it you haven't been home yet?" and I said, "No." "Oh well, when you get home there is a telegram waiting for you to ring Rod Smallwood because they're interested in you joining Iron Maiden."

'I said, "Well, how did they know about me?" She said Steve used to come down every night and watch the band play. I didn't know Steve at the time. He apparently loved it. Iron Maiden weren't allowed to play in the Bridge House club because they were too heavy. So they were over the Cart and Horses. On the nights they weren't playing and when he knew RDB were going to play the Bridge House, he would come down. Again one night I remember him in there because he had a West Ham scarf on and I was taking the mickey out of him.

'When I got home my wife said, "There's a telegram here for you," and I said, "I know what it is." And I picked up the telegram and it just said, "Dear Dennis, please ring Rod Smallwood at the above number re Iron Maiden." The following day I was down at Wardour Street, in the Ship pub near the Marquee, and I met up with Steve, Dave Murray and Rod. From there Rod said, "Steve wants you in the band. I don't think you will have any trouble learning the material."'

As excited as he was about the opportunity, Stratton also admitted that, heading into the gig, he was nervous because 'I was a bit ignorant about Iron Maiden's material at the time because I had been so involved with RDB and the tour with Quo. I had, therefore, never really got to listening to the really heavy metal stuff. And he said they had a really big following and they had done *The Soundhouse Tapes* but "we are due to go into the studio and record the first album" on EMI.

'He told me about this big following at the Soundhouse [club] and Neal Kay, [and that] they had signed this big deal with EMI. What they were looking for was not only a guitarist that could do backing vocals and whatever but someone who also had a bit of experience in the recording studios and touring because you have got to remember they were still very young. Although they had done lots of gigs in clubs and travelled around a lot in the old Green Goddess – they'd done one-night gigs up in Wigan and places – they had never actually done a full tour.

So I said, "Yeah, no problem." There was a little bit of an argument about money because I was married and had a little daughter, and I needed a bit more money than the rest of them because they were all living with their parents and whatever. So we got all that out of the way and they gave me a tape of some songs. I went home and I think the first one I played was "Phantom of the Opera", and it had all these harmonies and I thought, "Yeah, this is all right." They were rehearsing over at Hollywood Studios, Clapham, just round the corner from where Dave was living with his mum. I went over there and there was tons of gear, and I have never rehearsed so bloody loud in all my life. We went through a few harmony things and they were over the moon. They just said, "This is exactly what we have been looking for. You're in. Let's get going," and all that.

But in addition to replacing Paul Cairns, the band also needed a new beat-keeper following the departure of Doug Sampson. 'We went for a beer in the pub next door,' Stratton continued, 'and I was talking to Steve and Paul or Dave, and I said, "I didn't realise you were looking for a drummer." They were auditioning at the time and they had tried out Thundersticks [of Samson] and a few others, and they said, "Can you recommend anyone?"

'At the time I had played with two drummers. Johnny Richardson was an excellent drummer. Unfortunately, his hearing was playing up: he was told by the doctor that he couldn't carry on playing. If he did, he would end up deaf. The other drummer was Clive Burr. So I said, "There are a couple of drummers I know."

My preferred choice was Johnny Richardson. He was the best drummer – very technical, very clever and fast. He came down and gave it a go but he couldn't handle the volume. And he just said, "Sorry, Den, I can't do it."

'So I said, "There is one more person." I used to see Clive Burr over at the Fleece. It's a pub on Wanstead Flats that everyone goes to in the summer and they all sit outside. I saw him in there one night and I said, "What are you doing? I'm now working with Iron Maiden and they're looking for a drummer." And he said, "Well, stick my name forward." He came down to the rehearsal the next day and played, and they went, "Yeah, fine," and that is how he ended up coming in.'

With the line-up problem sorted out, attention turned to the material for the band's debut. One fascinating signature of Maiden's broader sound began from album one with Steve Harris's bass lines. 'I think the songs sound a bit different because they are written on the bass,' he told journalist John Stix. 'Some I write with a main bass riff and work out the melody on top of it. Some songs begin with a strong melody line and I work out the music behind it. I pretty much work everything out on the bass, the actual riffs and the harmonies ... Mainly they are little melodies, which have harmonies put to them.'

Giving fans an insight into his creative side, Harris added of his songwriting process that among his biggest challenges was assembling the many song sections he wrote individually into cohesive finished pieces, sharing in the same interview that, 'A lot of songs were written in different sections that could possibly have been used in other songs.'

Touching on some of his collaborative moments with his bandmates, Harris offered 'Remember Tomorrow' as an example. '[Singer] Paul Di'Anno wrote the lyrics to it. I wrote the music. Actually, I played him the parts I had and he worked it out. There's a lot of feeling in that song. Mind you, I think any song should be filled with feeling. But on the slow parts of this one I think there is that extra measure.'

'Charlotte the Harlot' the bassist happily acknowledged as 'Dave's song. I would have been proud to say that I'd written it. I like playing it live because it was something a bit different than I would write.'

The song's co-writer, Paul Di'Anno, told *Battle Helm* e-zine that the lyrics were actually autobiographical. '[Charlotte's] real name is High Hill Lil and she's basically an old prostitute. Well, actually she was more of a slut, ha ha. I mean, if you turned up to her house with some booze or some speed, you were more or less guaranteed a lay. She was a legend in Walthamstow, everyone knew her. She was about forty-five but a real rock-out bitch. She'd take any guy from fifteen upwards, ha ha! The song says that she lived on Acacia Avenue but it's actually Markhouse Road, just before you go into Leyton, 'cause that's the area where I lived.'

The singer added that 'Running Free' was equally autobiographical. '[It's] about me as a kid. My mum ruled my life but she said to me, "You live in a shit area but do what you can do and see what happens. As long as you don't hurt anybody, just get on with it." But I did get into trouble with the law a few times and that's the only thing I wish I could change – the grief I gave my poor mama. I never really knew my real dad but my step-dad was really cool. Sometimes he'd surprise us and walk in when we were doing some speed but he'd just brush it off as long as it wasn't heroin or the hard shit. I don't have the same attitude with my kids though – if I catch 'em with anything, I'll kick the crap outta them.'

Of the song's music, Harris added to Stix that '"Running Free" came together when I put a riff to the main drum beat by Doug Sampson. He was the drummer on *The Soundhouse Tapes*.' Guitarist Dennis Stratton would add later that the band were fond enough of the song to include it on their debut LP, recalling to *Praying Mantis*, 'We went back in and re-recorded "Running Free". It had to be a different mix and have different bits in it for radio play. It was the same with "Woman in Uniform".'

Citing the fan favourite 'Phantom of the Opera' as an example, Harris told Stix how he and his bandmates developed the musical side of the album's very long songs. As a result of its length, the song 'was done in sections. The middle part was totally separate but it fit in very well. It felt right to go from the slow part into the middle section.' The song would wind up as one of Harris' personal favourites. '"Phantom" is one of the best pieces I've ever written and certainly one of the most enjoyable to play. It's got all of these intricate guitar lines, which keep it interesting. Then there's that slow middle part, which creates quite a good mood. It's also got the fast heavy parts, which are really rockin'. And it's also got areas for crowd participation. It pretty much covers all the bases for the band. It was also a good example of what I wanted to get across.'

Billboard hailed the result as 'a landmark, the band's earliest progressive epic and still among its best. With its ambitious fusion of musical styles, its multi-sectioned construction and the literary retelling of the lyrics, it seemed to encapsulate all the promise of both the band and the New Wave of British Heavy Metal.'

Of 'Transylvania' – another signature of Iron Maiden's catalogue, the elaborate prog-metal instrumental – Harris would recall in the same interview that 'the initial idea on this one was to have lyrics. It originally had a melody line for the vocal but, when we played it, it sounded so good as an instrumental that we never bothered to write lyrics for it.'

In the opposite direction, the bassist singled out 'Strange World' as 'one of the only sort of slow songs we've done. But it's got a lot of feeling. It used to be a stage favourite. Dave [Murray] really enjoyed playing the solo in this one.'

Of another mainstay with the band's live audience – the title track – Harris recalled in the same interview – that for 'as long as I can remember we've closed our set with ["Iron Maiden"]. It's quite simple. The bass line is fairly straightforward, as is the drumming. But the guitar is over the top with harmony and the bass is descending behind it. I think this makes it pretty special.'

Guitarist Murray, a member of the band since 1976, quipped of the song that it had gone through several evolutions in line with the band's varying vocal line-ups prior to recording. In response to *Metal Hammer*'s question of 'who sings it the best?' he answered, 'No comment! Obviously, each singer has their own inflections but "Iron Maiden" was written and sung by vocalists before Paul

Di'Anno; it's only that he was the one to be heard singing it first.'

The band entered Kingsway Studios in London in February 1980. The studio has a rich recording history that includes Jimi Hendrix, Herman's Hermits, The Who, The Rolling Stones, Nazareth and T-Rex among others. It had been sold to Olympic in the mid-1970s but the studio's classic design and technical layout remained largely intact into the early 1980s.

Kingsway were also the first studio to buy one of Sound Techniques' legendary desks. According to Sound Techniques' website, 'Soon after the [Sound Techniques] studio opened [in Chelsea in 1964], word of the "Sound Techniques sound" spread to London's other independent studios. With this in mind, [founder] Geoff [Frost] designed and built the first customised Sound Techniques mixing desk, the A Range. By 1965 Kingsway studio in Holborn had purchased the first customised desk stamped with the Sound Techniques brand name. Trident Studios swiftly followed suit and purchased a desk, which was used to record the Beatles' "Hey Jude" and several of the *White Album* tracks, including "Martha My Dear" and "Dear Prudence". For the next ten years Sound Techniques desks were shipped out all over the world, from Hollywood to Jamaica.'

Years later *Billboard* would hail Stratton and Murray's guitar work recorded at Kingway, concluding that the pair 'explodes with energy and ideas' throughout. As Harris told journalist Stix, 'Most songs have a guitar solo in the middle. We've always tried to do things a little differently. We thought instead of a guitar solo we'd have a guitar break which would consist of guitar runs and harmonies.

Dennis Stratton talked to *Praying Mantis* about his contribution. 'When I joined Maiden, there weren't many harmony guitars going on in the band but, because I was just totally obsessed with harmony guitars, everything I did with Maiden, I just sat in the studio and put harmonies on. And it sort of took form, e.g. with 'Running Free' and 'Phantom of the Opera'. All them were harmony parts that I put loads of guitars on. And when we came to do the first Iron Maiden album, the engineer had me in the studio all day and night playing harmony guitars ... It was just in me and it made the two guitars sound different and a bit fuller. Rather than just playing chords while Dave [Murray] was playing, we did the two together.'

Vocally, the album broke new ground for heavy metal, an influence iTunes would acknowledge nearly three decades later. 'Lead singer Paul Di'Anno (who appears on this and *Killers*, the group's second album) has the shrieking and vibrato-emphasised vocal effects that became the standard for heavy-metal vocalists,' they noted.

Critics were equally impressed by the album's lush, layered backing vocals, which the BBC said were 'one of the high points of the album'. Highlighting one of his favourite harmony spots on the album – 'Phantom of the Opera' – Stratton told *Praying Mantis* that 'Paul did his lead vocal and I went in and did about four harmony parts on vocals, and built it right up. Rod Smallwood came into the control room and heard all these harmonies – it sounded huge – and he turned round and said, "It sounds like fucking Queen," and walked out. So half the vocals had to come off.'

Still, in sum, the parts that made up Iron Maiden's debut LP, released on 14 April 1980, would reshape and more importantly rehab a genre that had lost its way. The single 'Running Free' broke into the UK Top 40 singles chart and, as a consequence, the band was invited to perform on the BBC's important *Top of the Pops* show, offering them an opportunity to demonstrate that they were a group that called their own shots. Refusing to lip-synch the song, Iron Maiden became the first electric band since the Who seven years earlier to perform live before millions of Brits. It turned the band into an overnight metal sensation.

The band's next single, 'Sanctuary', reached No. 29 on the UK singles chart but was not included on the UK album (although it did appear on the US version, which hit the stores Stateside three months later, on 17 August 1980). Speaking about the 'Sanctuary' situation, Steve Harris explained years later to journalist John Stix that, 'It was done at the same time as the first album but we didn't release a single in the States, so we thought we'd add an extra track on the album. It's a rockin' number.'

Critics began a love affair with the band's debut LP on first listen. *Billboard* said '*Iron Maiden* was a game-changer when it appeared on the scene in 1980.' *Rolling Stone* declared that '*Iron Maiden*, the band's 1980 debut album for major label Capitol Records, was pure, unadulterated, screaming heavy metal,' and the BBC hailed the album as 'a classic'.

The album went on to peak at No. 4 in the UK album chart. Guitarist Dennis Stratton recalled years later in an interview with *Get Ready to Rock!* that 'the record company knew the album was gonna do well because of advanced orders ... It was nice to get great support everywhere we went.' The band, it could be said, was welcomed so readily because, as iTunes would observe years later, 'Iron Maiden's debut album contains the beginnings of a new revolution within the heavy-metal community.' As *Billboard* would note, 'that year also saw important albums from Motörhead, Saxon and Angel Witch ... [but] *Iron Maiden* vaulted its creators to the head of the New British Wave of Heavy Metal's pack.'

Decades after its original release, critics like *Classic Rock* magazine would continue to say that 'Iron Maiden's debut album [is] also their best ... In comparison with the sleek prog-metal machine the band evolved into, *Iron Maiden* sees them as a bunch of scruffy East End herberts with a powerful point to prove. That signature Steve Harris bass sound is there from the start and singer Paul Di'Anno is on prime form. Bruce Dickinson might try his damnedest but songs such as "Prowler" and "Charlotte the Harlot" just aren't the same without Di'Anno's growl. Much has been made of Maiden's punk influences but, in truth, *Iron Maiden* is just an aggressive metal album and as raw as an open wound.'

Years later Di'Anno would tell *Battle Helm* e-zine that 'I loved the first album [because] ... it was more punky.' Critically, Di'Anno's vocal work on the band's debut has held up over the years compared to the band's broader catalogue. As *Billboard* observed, '*Iron Maiden* would still rank as a landmark even if the Dickinson years had never happened.'

CHAPTER TWO

KILLERS (1981)

'Maiden was Steve's baby'
Paul Di'Anno

Heading into their second LP Iron Maiden were in the right place at the right time to lead the second British wave of metal. The band laid down *Killers* between November 1980 and January 1981 at Battery Studios in London with producer Martin Birch, whose credits included a virtual who's who of 1970s rock stars, from the Faces to Deep Purple and from Blue Oyster Cult to Black Sabbath.

Amusingly, Birch later quipped to VH1's *Classic Albums* that 'I read they were going to go into the studio and do an album, and I was a bit peeved because I wondered, "Well, why they haven't asked me?" because I was interested in doing it.' To which Steve Harris responded in the same show that, 'We didn't approach him because we thought he was unapproachable at that point. He was this big star producer and we thought he wouldn't be interested in this small band.'

Once the band and producer were on the same page,

Killers would mark the first stage in what would be a long collaboration. In an interview with *Best* magazine the producer said of the prospect of working with Maiden that 'I personally wanted to produce them because it was a way out of the Purple family. There are, in fact, many differences. Musically, a band like Iron Maiden is typical of the second generation of hard rock and stands out from the first one because the band is more consistent, more compact.'

In the same conversation Birch recalled his impressions of working with the band. 'At first, I could judge them objectively and I think that they are very different from the hard rockers of the early 1970s ... The first time I saw them at work I was surprised, and seduced by their energy and their attitude. I have rarely seen bands with so much energy. In this way, they reminded me a bit of the early Purple. But their attitude towards rock is very different and so is their concept of it. It was said that they were a second Deep Purple but I don't agree with this. Obviously Steve Harris was a Purple fan but he's mostly influenced by bands like Jethro Tull, UFO or even Genesis. Nothing to do with Deep Purple. Of course, in both cases we have a very melodic hard rock and not just speeded-up noise like with some other bands in heavy metal.'

Though the group was working with such a storied UK producer – known affectionately among the bands he has produced as 'The Headmaster' – Harris told IronMaiden.com that creating the record began and ended as a team effort. 'I appreciate that someone from outside of the band can see different things [but] there has to be some form of internal control. If I heard something that I felt was vital to Iron Maiden, I would be after that guy. But even then it would still have to be a co-production affair because I've always insisted upon that right from when we started working with Martin Birch on *Killers*.'

Birch, for his part, was easily agreeable to this arrangement, quite simply because – as he recalled to *Best* – from the outset of entering the studio it was 'obvious that he's the boss, even if he denies it himself. Iron Maiden – that's him. Moreover, the situation of the band made that, for a long time, all the songwriting was down to him.'

But while Harris received credit as the band's principal songwriter, he was consistently generous in giving credit to his bandmates for their contributions. Of guitarist Dave Murray and the composition 'Twilight Zone', for example, he said, 'This was a single in England that wasn't on the British album. We put it on as an extra track over here [the US]. Dave came up with the riff for this one. I wrote the melody line and the lyrics. But the main riff was Dave's.'

Harris also seemed to be the first to appreciate the writing of new guitarist Adrian Smith, who had replaced Dennis Stratton, and singled out 'Wrathchild' as an instance where the guitarist had contributed to improving the song. '"Wrathchild" was originally recorded on an album called *Metal for Muthas*, along with "Sanctuary",' he told Ironmaidencommentary.com. 'That was before we had a record contract. The version on this record is pretty different. A lot of people asked us why we didn't put it on the first album but we felt, because it was on *Metal for Muthas*, we didn't want to put it on the first album. By the time we did *Killers* we weren't happy with that version so we wanted to record it properly. The guitar frills around the vocals were from Adrian. Originally they weren't there but, when Adrian joined the band, he decided to put them in.'

Addressing the pressures of his role as songwriter-in-chief at that point in the band's fledgling career, Harris readily volunteered to rock journalist Johnny B that 'any type of songwriting is never particularly easy. Just coming up with new ideas and new material and everything is always quite a lot of pressure.'

As he went about writing the album, Steve shared in the same conversation that 'I try and grab inspiration from wherever I can ... Thank you very much. I grab it with both hands. Obviously you do get ideas at funny times and you just have to write them down. Sometimes it can be weird as you can put down an idea and then, when you look back at it a few weeks later, you think it is not as good as you thought it was, or other ideas then seem better than you originally thought they were. Usually, however, when you have got a strong one, you have a gut feeling on it but it is always a worry as to whether it is as good as you think. I think it is the biggest pressure of all as it is a personal thing.'

As production on the album got underway, a key element involved rearranging older Maiden songs that hadn't made it on to the debut LP. This allowed Harris and company the opportunity to improve both the writing and sonics of these cuts. In conversation with Ironmaidencommentary.com, the chief songwriter singled out 'Innocent Exile' as 'one of the very first Iron Maiden songs. It was an old stage favourite but we haven't played it in a while. That opening bass riff was originally played on the guitar. It was written on the bass for the guitar. The bass was originally playing crashing chords behind it. Then we switched it around.'

Harris also cited 'Purgatory' as 'quite an old song' that the band had reworked in a slightly different form. 'It was originally called "Floating". Then we changed the lyrics and a couple of bits in the middle section.'

Of the title track, 'Killers', Harris recalled that 'Paul [Di'Anno] wrote the lyrics to that one. It felt really natural for him to scream at the start of the song.' In the case of 'Drifter', Harris highlighted the stylistic diversity of the band members' influences as they blended in collaboration. 'The different parts in this song really flowed together ... The slow section in there is one of Dave's blues things ... It wasn't a song that was done in separate sections. On this one I pretty much knew what I wanted.'

Another musical signature of the band was introduced on *Killers* – their now legendary instrumental. This, All Music Guide explained, began with producer Martin Birch 'beefing up the band's studio presence and lending their instrumental attack a newfound clarity that throws their considerable skills into sharp relief'. Offering 'Genghis Khan' as an example, Steve Harris told Ironmaidencommentary.com that the band's decision to record the song as an instrumental initially 'freaked out' Birch. 'It was sort of a change at right angles. We really liked that element of surprise. This was another song where there could have been a vocal melody on top but it felt good as an instrumental. A vocal would have cluttered it up. Originally it was written to depict the feeling and sound of Genghis Khan's army going into battle.'

Harris also highlighted 'Murders in the Rue Morgue' as another example of an album track that wound up as 'a bit of an experiment'. 'I'd never played harmonics on the bass much before that. But, with the mood of the intro, it felt really natural to play those harmonics. We wanted to create a mood, and then come in and hit people across the head with it. The vocal melody is pretty much the same as the riff. That's to give them both more power.'

As the album began taking shape, Harris – who had expressed some dissatisfaction with the production on the band's debut – told Ironmaidencommentary.com that, while 'the first album really sounded like a first album, with *Killers* we started to sound more like Maiden. It was the first album where we felt some satisfaction as far as the sound of the album.'

For his part, producer Birch explained to *Best* magazine of his more successful production style that 'I don't consider myself a super-technician – what I do is, to me, pretty simple.'

On its release in the UK in February 1981 *Killers* reached No. 12 on the Top 20 Album Chart. From the band's point of view, Steve Harris selected the title cut and "Murders in the Rue Morgue" as 'two songs [that] stand out because they are great live favourites.' Four months later, in June, the album was released in the US, reaching No. 68 – a big improvement on its predecessor's peak of No. 124. *Billboard* hailed the album as 'clearly the work of a top-notch ensemble' and boldly stated that 'the teaming of new guitarist Adrian Smith with Dave Murray [formed] the most formidable twin-guitar attack in heavy metal'.

CHAPTER THREE

THE NUMBER OF THE BEAST (1982)

'Exemplary displays of the group's instrumental prowess, their uncanny knack for writing accessible riffs without pandering to the commercial marketplace and the perfect launch pad for Dickinson's commanding operatic vocal style ... There isn't a weak track here'
iTunes LP review

'You are trying to create some sort of mood or image with the imagery of the songs, I suppose. They're all short stories and come from all different influences' Steve Harris

'This would be the ideal candidate for your first Iron Maiden album' BBC

For years Iron Maiden fans, peers and critics have debated the importance of *The Number of the Beast* in shaping both Maiden's career as metal trailblazers and the face of heavy metal overall. Years later iTunes would conclude that 'future metal musicians – especially in the underground scenes of thrash, death and black metal – would refer to Maiden's intricate twin-guitar weavings and rhythmic overkill for their own unrelenting attack. [*The Number of the Beast* is] a heavy-metal essential from every angle.'

Before heading into the studio to record their third LP Iron Maiden faced a dilemma following the exit of their front man Paul Di'Anno. As the BBC put it, 'Given the importance people attach to the role of the vocalist in rock groups, the upward curve that Iron Maiden had steadily enjoyed since their first album in 1980 might well have become a downward spiral with the departure of singer Paul Di'Anno. Echoing Spinal Tap's legendary problems in keeping their drummers, he was already the third singer since their humble beginnings as a pub band.'

With the benefit of hindsight, years later Di'Anno would confess to *Battle Helm* e-zine that, 'To be frank, at that age I wasn't ... handling things as well as the other guys, who were older than me. One minute I was a kid off the street and the next I was expected to handle things like it was sliced bread. Needless to say, I started drinking a lot and I must've done half of Peru up my nose. I screwed up ... I wasn't happy, both with the album and myself, and I really didn't wanna be there. And if you can't give a thousand per cent to a band like Iron Maiden, the best thing to do is get the fuck out. I just walked in and told them how I felt and walked away.'

Di'Anno has been more or less diplomatic over the years about the true reasons he left, though these range from his comment to *Classic Rock* that 'I left Iron Maiden because they were going too heavy metal and Iron Maiden is a money-making machine, and I don't give a fuck about it,' to his claim in the same interview that he left because of creative constraints. 'Iron Maiden is Steve Harris's band. It doesn't matter about anybody else – whether it's Dave Murray, Clive [Burr], me ... it's Steve Harris's band.'

To *Ultimate Metal* magazine Di'Anno was more specific, from a musical perspective, saying, 'I think Bruce's high operatic and theatrical-type voice is better suited to Maiden's later material.' Ultimately, however, he concluded that, 'there are still a lot of people who seem to forget that my voice was and still is a huge part of Maiden's past, and I am both happy and proud of that fact.'

To take the next step forward Maiden's musical ambitions clearly required a vocalist as technically accomplished as the band. Enlisted to replace Di'Anno was Samson front man Bruce Dickinson. After an audition in September 1981 he recalled in an interview with *Billboard* that the move to front Maiden made sense because 'we effectively grew up together, musically, because I was in Samson and all the bands were aware of everybody else. We all gigged together. It's fair to say Maiden had this momentum about them. It was like standing in front of a truck...

'Things with Paul hadn't been going terribly well and they'd made the decision to get rid of him. So they came and took a peek at me. Clive [Burr, then Maiden's drummer] had been in Samson for three years and *Killers* was being made at Zomba Studios [in London], which back then was Morgan Studios ... We were in Morgan and Maiden were in the [studio] opposite so we used to go to the pub, and have a few beers and chat. I went over and listened to the Maiden record, and Clive would come over and listen to ours ... Rod Smallwood offered me the chance of an audition – he didn't offer me the job – at Reading Festival.'

Already well aware of Steve Harris's locally legendary role as the band's head songwriter, Dickinson also recalled clarifying the terms of any potential collaboration from the outset. '"First of all," I said, "if I do the audition, I'm going to get the job so you need to figure out whether or not you want me onboard because I don't want to be unless I can be a pain in the ass and have some opinions. I'm not going to be like the old guy. I'm going to have disagreements with Steve because I've got some ideas about how I want to change things around. So if you don't want that, you'd better tell me now."

'They asked me to learn three songs and I basically learned the lot, both albums. So we turned up to the rehearsal room and let rip. Steve picked up the phone and said, "Could we get him into a studio today?" They were still doing gigs with Paul. The atmosphere was a bit down. When they came back from Sweden, we popped in the studio, recorded three songs and that was it. That was job done. We all went out and got very drunk that night.'

The band's decision to hire Dickinson, as the BBC would conclude, 'turned out to be fourth time lucky for them. And for Dickinson, whose sandpapered soaring yowl more than held its own against the blasting and frequently bombastic arrangements.' Producer Martin Birch added his unequivocal opinion to *Best* magazine: 'It's certain that Bruce Dickinson has improved the band as compared with Paul Di'Anno, who was isolated at the human level and who wasn't very productive.'

Addressing the question of how the line-up changes affected the group musically, Steve Harris explained to *Artist* magazine that 'on the *Killers* album Adrian was very new and it really wasn't until he'd been with the band about a year and a half that he really felt he was a full member. He always had been but he never really seemed to accept that it was happening. [Perhaps] because he went from a local band in the East End to Iron Maiden, which, even at the time, was quite a big act. It took him quite a while to settle in, and it also took both him and Dave a long time to get the right guitar sounds ... Then Bruce came in and he really did fine things for the band too.'

As the band faced up to recording their new album Steve Harris confessed in an interview with VH1's *Classic Albums* that 'we had no material'. As he explained to journalist Kevin Purcell, 'On the first two albums we had a lot of material lying around from before we got signed. On the third album [*The Number of the Beast*] there was absolutely nothing, and we had a specific period of time to write and a load of pressure to write.' Instead of inviting disaster, however, Harris said, 'It worked great.' Setting a precedent that became the band's norm thereafter, he reasoned that, 'If you were to allow yourself a year to write, you would get distracted and do a lot of other stuff in between. When you're stuck into it, you get to it.'

Identified by the BBC as 'a key weapon' in crafting the album, Harris detailed to *Classic Albums* the band's writing process. 'Some of the simpler songs are written in minutes, literally. It sounds a strange thing to say but they're written quite quickly and some songs – some of our best and catchiest – do work like that.'

Of the band's longer compositions – a strength that the BBC hailed as a 'convincing use of multi-movement composition' – Bruce Dickinson recalled in the same interview, 'Steve likes to go off and do all his stuff on his own and plan it all out.'

Harris concurred, adding his agreement that those are 'ones you have to work on, especially the longer ones ... If I'm writing a song and if it's just got my name on it, usually I've written everything except for the guitar solos.'

When he did introduce his compositions for the album to his bandmates, Harris pointed out another unique difference between Iron Maiden and their metal contemporaries. 'I just take it to the rest of the guys, show them the parts and just sort of layer it out like that. We don't do demos and stuff.'

His bandmates then worked on helping one another flesh out the songs' live feel. As guitarist Adrian Smith explained in the same VH1 show, 'You take a rough idea in and that's a great thing about being in a band because, from your seed of an idea, it becomes this big-sounding track. That's one of the thrills for me of doing it, to actually get in the studio and record it properly.'

Talking to journalist John Stix about some of the collaborative efforts on the album, Harris began with 'Gangland', proudly crediting the song as having been written by 'Adrian and Clive. The intro is very much a drum thing, which Clive got together. It's probably a bit jazz-influenced and a bit different than things we'd done before. But the basic riff is very much a rocker. It's a very good song.'

Another group effort, 'The Prisoner', was praised by the BBC. '[Where] even some of the venerable HM institutions (think Black Sabbath) would struggle to make material that was something more than a collection of minor-key riffs, Iron Maiden pull this feat off with considerable élan. "The Prisoner" could almost pass for a heavy-metal Genesis.'

For the band, the most memorable aspect of creating this song came with its introduction, as Bruce Dickinson told VH1's *Classic Albums*. 'Obviously we wanted to be really sort of dramatic with the intro so we thought, "Well, maybe we can snip the intro off *The Prisoner* TV series." Steve Harris added, 'It was quite funny because we had to get permission from Patrick McGoohan for the intro to "Prisoner" and we didn't actually realise at the time he owned the rights to it all. So Rod, our manager, had to actually get on to him personally about it.'

Smallwood recalled a somewhat botched call followed in which he tried to explain exactly what the band wanted to use the intro for. 'After a pregnant pause of around five seconds he said, "Do it." For people who know McGoohan, that's very Patrick McGoohan!'

Turning to the album opener, 'Invaders', Steve Harris explained to journalist Stix that 'this song was an extension of another song called "Invasion", which was the B-side of the single "Women in Uniform". It's like an invasion of

Britain ... [It] felt like a great rock 'n' roll opener. "Children of the Damned" is next on the album. It's based on the film of the same name. The mood was sort of like "Remember Tomorrow".'

Of the album's title track and fan favourite, Steve Harris said, 'Basically that song is about a dream. It's not about Devil worship ... The idea was to get a blood-curdling scream like the one on "Won't Get Fooled Again". It worked quite well.' Addressing head on the rumours that the Christian Right had begun accusing the band of being involved with Satanism, he added, 'It was nothing to do with the 666 thing; that was exaggerated. We had loads of things going wrong. We had to get a completely different tape machine because it wasn't recording the stuff properly as it was going down. But I mean, those sorts of things can happen. It's just that we had more of it this time than any other time.'

'Run to the Hills', Harris explained to Stix, 'is about the American Indians. It's written from both sides of the picture. The first part is from the side of the Indians. The second part is from the side of the soldiers.' To VH1's *Classic Albums* he added that 'it's just basically about the Indian nations being treated badly and taken over really'. Homing in on the song's rhythms, which producer Martin Birch explained were designed to give listeners 'that rolling feel, that galloping feel', Harris added in the same conversation with Stix, 'I wanted to try and get the feeling of galloping horses. But, when you play this one, be careful not to let it run away with you.'

Following up the fan favourite 'Charlotte the Harlot' from the band's debut, the sequel '22 Acacia Avenue' was, Harris told Styx, quite simply 'an extension ... This is where she's living in London's East End.' He also identified this song as one of his personal favourites on the record, along with 'Hallowed Be Thy Name' and the title tune.

'Children of the Damned' took the classic horror film as its muse, as Harris told *Classic Albums.* '[Just] as most of our things are really loosely based on anything ... it was kind of based loosely on the movie, I suppose ... We just take a basic idea and then develop it from there really, and try to put our own twists and turns into it.'

Finally, 'Hallowed Be Thy Name', he revealed to Ironmaidencommentary.com years later, remains 'one of my favourite songs and still one we play live. We're trying to create a mood with the build-up of the song. The classical guitar-like opening was Dave building the mood, with bells in the background. It's about someone with only a few hours left to live. In concert the end part of this one takes off. Dave takes the first solo and then Adrian.'

As pre-production wrapped, producer Martin Birch confirmed Harris's central role in visualising what became British heavy metal's most influential concept album of the 1980s. Harris, he told *Best* magazine, had to keep both hands on the creative reigns. 'Adrian Smith and Bruce Dickinson needed some time to settle down. As for Dave Murray, who's an excellent guitar player, well, he doesn't write that much. He writes very little and he's very demanding. For *The Number of the Beast*, for example, everything was down to Steve.'

The admiration was mutual. 'By the time he did *Beast*,' Harris told *Classic Albums*, 'that was it really. He became our full-time producer and we didn't think about using anyone else.'

Ensconced again in Battery Studios they worked through tracking each of the album's tracks. Years later Clive Burr would share his opinion that 'every song really had something about it that you could say, "Yeah, that part, this part, the whole of it, really worked well."'

Dissecting the sound that the band captured live during those sessions, KNAC.com would conclude that 'Iron Maiden is a metal band built around the power guitar chords. With guitarists like Murray and Smith this comes as no surprise but what sets Maiden apart is the use of their rhythm section. Where most metal bands keep their bassist in the background to keep the beat and use their drummer as a point of attack, Maiden does the opposite. Steve Harris uses the bass to lead the attack while their drummer keeps the rhythm.'

Feeling that it was the band's signature layered guitar sound that set them apart from many metal contemporaries, Steve Harris said to *Classic Albums*, 'You've got those twin guitars – it's just a trademark with Maiden. That's what we try to do, use all those elements.'

Harris also paid Dickinson a major compliment, telling *Artist* magazine that, during tracking, the singer was 'so quick in the studio because his ear for pitch is so good. He just gets up there and bang! It retains a great live feel.'

For his part, Dickinson told *Billboard* that the band had

'matured massively ... the sound of the band ... [after] Adrian joined and was writing'.

As principal recording wound down Harris recalled feeling that this was 'certainly the best-sounding Iron Maiden album, I must admit, but then we have spent a long time on it. I would much rather work this way; maybe not spend quite so long. But at the end of the day it sounds like the best thing we've ever done.'

Everyone seemed to know they were on to something truly special. As manager Rod Smallwood recalled to *Classic Albums*, 'There was a certain excitement on *The Number of the Beast,* 'cause we all felt – me especially – that there was something special about that album. Just the way it was coming together, the songs, the addition of Bruce, the extra scope we had to work with. There was a certain feeling on that album that it was something special.'

Dickinson agreed, reflecting that his first LP with the band 'sounded completely new – people had never heard anything quite like it before'.

Producer Martin Birch also chipped in, telling *Best*, 'It's true that it's a band whose line-up changes quite a lot ... [but it's] a good thing in this case, as each newcomer brings a certain amount of freshness to each album.'

Steve Harris, too, described a 'feeling of excitement and aggression ... when we went from *Killers* to *The Number of the Beast*'. It was a buzz that was shared by fans and critics alike. According to iTunes, Harris had 'caught lightning in a bottle with an entire collection of tunes that became cornerstones of the Maiden catalogue'. The

BBC hailed the album as 'brilliant', advising 'Maiden newbies' to 'start their journey to metal hell and back right here'. Iron Maiden's journey, according to *Rolling Stone*, would take them to the top of the charts in Britain, initiating 'a streak of seven consecutive platinum or gold albums in the United States, despite virtually no radio or MTV exposure'.

On worldwide release on 29 March 1982, the band's achievement was remarkable, considering guitarist Dave Murray's memory that 'there were very few radio stations that were playing the band'. In the same interview with *Classic Albums* he added, 'Basically we had to go out there on tour and, hence, we go everywhere – East Coast, West Coast and everywhere in between.'

Echoing his client, manager Smallwood recalled in the same interview, 'We never got airplay so Maiden built completely by touring, not by a song being a hit and being on the radio.'

Happily for the band, they were pushing a sound that metal fans the world over had been waiting for in their millions. *The Number of the Beast* propelled the band not only to their first No. 1 on the UK album chart, where it remained within the Top 75 for over 30 weeks, but it broke them in America, where it reached the Top 40 of *Billboard*'s Top 200 Album Chart. Burning like wildfire up charts around the globe, the album went on to crack the Top 10 in Austria and Sweden, and the Top 20 in Canada and Norway. It also produced two Top 20 singles in the UK: 'Run to the Hills', which peaked at No. 7, and 'The Number of the Beast', which reached No. 18.

After just two albums with the band producer Martin Birch told *Best*, 'I am now as comfortable with Iron Maiden as I was in the best moments of Deep Purple.' What he added was music to Maiden fans' ears – he and Maiden had 'agreed to work together again for the next album!'

CHAPTER FOUR

PIECE OF MIND (1983)

'Iconic slab of metal'
Classic Rock Revisited

'Usually the numbers are better live than on record. That has to do with the feel of the songs. Most of them were written to be played on the stage. They're not really for the recording studio' Steve Harris

Following up the wild success of *Number of the Beast*, Iron Maiden had, indeed, achieved some piece of mind by 1983, choosing it as the title of their fourth studio album in as many years. Twenty-five years later it would be hailed by metal internet radio station KNAC.com as 'the greatest album in the history of civilisation'.

Heading into recording, Steve Harris felt the band was at their strongest yet musically, primarily due to what he cited as the 'really big difference' the band's new drummer Nicko McBrain was making. 'His drumming is some of the best rock drumming there is,' Harris told *Artist* magazine. 'His feel is magic. Nicko toured with us when he played with the French band Trust in 1981 and 1982 so he's been on the road with us. Trust and Iron Maiden have always been big friends anyway and personality-wise there was no problem. He was actually born about a mile and a half from me and he's just a couple of years older than I am.'

Delving into how he felt McBrain's unique brand of skin-hitting had strengthened Maiden's metal precision, the bassist said, 'His drumming, I think, has given us a different dimension. It's tougher and his timing is perfect. He's a total rock drummer; he's got a great feel and he hits it real hard. So the whole thing has grown up. Every album has improved both in term of production and musicianship. I think now it's really becoming what Iron Maiden is all about and we expect it's going to develop even more from here.'

Concurring, producer Martin Birch added in a conversation with *Best* magazine that, on '*Piece Of Mind*, the contribution of Nicko [McBrain] was tremendous. He really is a great drummer.'

Harris volunteered candidly to journalist Johnny B that the most challenging part of diving into the making of any new studio LP, for him, was that 'coming up with new material is always the most stressful thing and the biggest worry. You have standards – both yours and others' – that you want to meet and yet you don't want to repeat yourself because what's the point of that? I think some bands do try and repeat themselves, and do try and recreate the success that they had from one particular album ... We don't do that, we have never tried to do that. If anything, we tried to do stuff that we have never created before. We wanna do stuff that is different, new and refreshing for us and [our fans].'

Speaking of the band's camaraderie throughout the writing process, producer Birch told *Best*, 'Even within the band, although Steve Harris is the boss because he founded it and writes most of the songs, there is a great unity and nobody tries to stand out individually from the team. It's really nice and mostly really exciting because their music is full of energy.'

Even though the band had attained global fame by this point thanks to the smash success of *The Number of the Beast*, Birch recalled that the band kept grounded and focused on maintaining their signature sound in the studio. 'They don't fall into easy – and very boring – solutions with tewenty-minute guitar solos, then keyboards, then drums, like I experienced with Deep Purple,' he told *Best*. 'I think they're more robust, musically speaking. Another difference is their attitude towards the outside world. They are not into the "star system" and remain very accessible. Success has not raised any barriers between them and the others, press, audience.'

Compass Point Studios, built by Island Records' founder Chris Blackwell in Nassau, Bahamas, is described on its official website as offering artists 'the opportunity to create in an environment where they first rise in the morning for a swim in the warm tropical waters. Stroll or jog along a beautiful beach. Enjoy a gourmet breakfast under a palm covered verandah. Then make the short walk to one of the world's most famous, spacious and well-equipped studios to begin your day's work. Any time you need a break, just step outside and gaze across an endless seascape of ocean blue, breathe in the fresh sea air and then come back refreshed.

'When the day's work is finished, leisurely stroll home

under a canopy of brilliant stars. Compass Point Studios in Nassau, Bahamas, have been the "Home Studio to the Stars" now for 33 years. The history of what has been recorded here is virtually unmatched in the industry.'

Continuing, the studio adds of its legendary history that, as it attracted a diverse array of musical sub-genres in the form both of reggae legends like Bob Marley and harder rock acts like AC/DC and, finally, metal bands like Iron Maiden, 'in the late 1970s and mid-1980s, Compass Point was one of the great recording studios of the world. Artists came from around the world to record in the Bahamas. Many major producers utilised the facilities, including Chris Blackwell himself, in his role as record producer. The resulting records sold in the many millions of copies worldwide. AC/DC's *Back in Black*, widely regarded as the ultimate and largest-selling rock album of all time, was just one of the many great albums recorded at Compass Point Studios.'

Qualifying the studio's rich history of recorded diversity, a review of only a handful of the legends Compass Point has attracted over the years includes none other than The Rolling Stones, U2, Robert Palmer, The B-52's, Talking Heads, Dire Straits, Bob Marley, Eric Clapton, The Cure, Adam Ant, James Brown, Duran Duran, David Bowie, Judas Priest, Mick Jagger, Whitesnake, ELO, Status Quo, Tom Tom Club, Joe Cocker, Emerson Lake and Palmer, Eurythmics, Power Station, Roxy Music, Wings, Ringo Starr, Julian Lennon, Bad Company and many others.

According to founder/owner Blackwell, 'I decided to build a studio in a restful location ... and I built it from scratch. A man who worked at the studio at Island's offices in London was the sound designer and he created a magic room.' Elaborating more on the technical side of the studio's construction, journalist David Katz explained that '[Blackwell had] conceived Compass Point as a giant blank canvas for audio, a space where music could be made without the distraction of external influence.

'Construction of the 24-track facility took place in 1977, with an MCI 500 series mixing desk and other top-notch equipment installed, initially in one room. High-profile recording sessions took place almost from its very inception: in March and April 1978, Talking Heads made the first of many appearances there to record *More Songs about Buildings and Food*. 1979 began with Dire Straits' second album, *Communique* and, immediately after, the Rolling Stones were in residence for a month to work on *Tattoo You*.

'In fact, so many mainstream rock acts were booking the place that Blackwell had to build Studio B, a second recording room, to ensure enough time was available for his own projects. It was towards the end of 1979 that Compass Point really came into its stride.'

Rolling Stones guitarist Keith Richards offered of the studio's magic live vibe that 'a lot of Jamaican reggae interests me because they have a lovely, wide-open concept about recording, which the rest of us are slowing coming around to. For them, a console is as much an instrument as a drum or a guitar ... They'll just go "Whack! Bang!" and drop out an instrument.'

Bruce Dickinson described the band's recording process

there to journalist Robert Jock as one where the group tracked live together off the floor, seeking to maintain the consistency of the energy of their live performances in the studio as they were onstage, explaining, 'All the early Maiden records were always recorded in sort of traditional fashion where, yes, you play the stuff but the drummer goes and gets his parts right, then everybody else goes in and they play their bits over the top, and you build it up in layers.'

The album's opener is 'Where Eagles Dare', of which KNAC concluded, 'The guitars are perfect, as Adrian Smith and Dave Murray launch one of several incredible guitar solos ... and solos that feature gunfire in the background. The bass is surprisingly low key and Maiden even decides to use the drums a little bit differently than they normally do.'

Steve Harris recalled to Ironmaidencommentary.com, 'It's supposed to sound like a machine gun. It's not very loud in the mix but we wanted it that way so people who listened to it a couple of times would say, "What's that?" That song was done in two takes.'

Of 'Die With Your Boots On,' Harris recalled a group collaboration. 'Adrian and Bruce came up with the main riff. Bruce came up with the lyrics. I came up with the chord sequence behind the verse and the cross section that goes into the main chorus. This is another personal favourite of mine. It has more chords than riffs, which I suppose might make it strange as to why I really like it so much. It's a very powerful number live. I get off on the aggression of it.'

Turning to the creation of 'Still Life', the bassist said, 'It's basically a story of a guy who is drawn like a magnet to a pool of water. He sees faces in the lake. He has nightmares about it and, in the end, he jumps in and takes his lady with him. It's a very enjoyable number to play because there's a lot going on. Again we're creating a mood and coming in with a very heavy guitar sound. Adrian takes the first solo. After the solo there is a really tight bass-and-drums staccato part, which goes right across the top of the riff. I like that part a lot.'

Discussing the double meaning in the lyrics of 'The Trooper', Harris explained that, on one level, 'basically it's an answer to the religious freaks for giving us such a hard time on *The Number of the Beast*', adding that, on another level, it was 'based on the Crimean war with the British against the Russians. The opening is meant to try and recreate the galloping horses in the charge of the Light Brigade. It's an atmospheric song.'

'Revelations' was a song that KNAC concluded 'brings out one of Maiden's strengths – having two great guitarists with the talent to share/swap the rhythm and lead guitar duties and go back and forth on the solos'. Harris recalled of its writing, 'That's Bruce's [song]. To me it's sort of a heavy version of the Wishbone Ash feel ... Bruce and myself are [also] very big Jethro Tull fans.'

Of other collaborations with the singer, the bass player singled out 'Sun and Steel', telling IronMaidenCommentary.com, 'Bruce wrote the lyrics to that. It's basically about a Japanese guy who builds himself up to a peak of fitness and wants to kill himself hara-kiri style. I think it would be a good live song but we have never played it on stage as of yet.'

'To Tame a Land' Harris identified as 'the best song I've ever written'. KNAC also sang its praise by arguing that 'whenever Maiden's epic saga songs get mentioned, it's usually referring to "Rime of the Ancient Mariner", "Alexander the Great" or even "Phantom of the Opera". Usually overlooked is the best of the bunch – that's right, "To Tame a Land".'

Bruce Dickinson, in the same conversation with IronMaidenCommentary.com, explained that this one is 'all about a gentleman who wrote a science-fiction book called *Dune*. He's an American called Mr Frank Herbert, this particular gentleman, all right? And Mr Herbert, as it turns out, is a bit of a cunt actually because ... among other things he said that if we called this track "Dune", he'd sue us and stop the album coming out, and all kinds of very unpleasant things ... So we had to re-title the track ... and we had to call it "To Tame a Land".'

For the song's author, the song marked a musical accomplishment he summed up by saying that 'I was really pleased with "Phantom" but now I have to say this is the best'. While he was happy with the majority of the album, Harris singled out 'Flight of Icarus' as a song that, 'looking back on it now, we feel we could have played ... at the faster speed on the album. This little extra touch gives it a bit more fire.'

Centering in on what producer Martin Birch brought to what many consider to be Iron Maiden's most important and influential album, Harris explained in a 1983 conversation with *Artist* magazine that 'the reason we use Martin is that he puts down the sound that we want, the way we like it. And we think the first three albums were really leading up to this one in terms of quality. In general, bands are being given producers that make the music for them and, in some cases, even co-write it. With Martin, that's not the case at all and never has been.'

In explaining why he felt the producer was continually ideal for the band, Harris offered, 'what Martin has always added with us is his expertise in the studio and his great ability at recording our sounds. We've only just come to this point in our drum and guitar sounds, which are exceptional now; it's just a team growing up together. Martin's also become aware, obviously, with the experience of working with us, of the way we want to proceed. The suggestions going both ways are very fluid so Martin's very much a part of the band in the studio.'

Released worldwide on 16 May 1983, *Piece of Mind* shot to No. 3 on the UK Top 20 album chart and No. 70 on the *Billboard* Top 200 album chart. It also produced the hit singles 'Flight of Icarus', which peaked at No. 8 on the *Billboard* Top Album Tracks chart, marking the highest position of any in the band's US chart history, and 'The Trooper', which peaked at No. 28 on the US Mainstream Rock charts.

Critics and fans alike held the album up high, with Popmatters.com years later declaring the album a 'classic', while *Kerrang!* published a poll in 1983 that declared *Piece of Mind* No. 1 on their Greatest Metal Albums of All Time list. A KNAC reviewer raved that the album was 'my favourite album of all time'.

For Steve Harris, the personal-highlight moments from the album included 'The Trooper' and 'Die With Your Boots On'. He told IronMaidenCommentary.com, 'Both are very good live numbers and, in the case of "The Trooper", because we managed to capture the right mood for the song.'

For Martin Birch, reflecting years later on his catalogue of collaborations with Iron Maiden, the producer – like most fans and critics – felt that the band's accomplishment with *Piece Of Mind* made it 'by far their best album'.

CHAPTER FIVE

POWERSLAVE (1984)/ LIVE AFTER DEATH (1985)

'Powerslave is frequently ranked as the fan favourite of the bunch' All Music Guide

'"Aces High" is about as perfect a heavy-metal tune as there is. It's about the Battle of Britain, told from the perspective of a British pilot' The National Review

Of the band's fifth studio LP, *Powerslave*, *Billboard* magazine would note that it represented 'the third in a trilogy of legendary Iron Maiden albums' and rounded out 'a stellar run that sealed the band's genre-defining status'. *Metal Observer* would hail it years later as 'another milestone' and even the traditionally conservative political magazine *National Review* was sonically smitten, celebrating it in a retrospective as the band's 'best album!' *Rolling Stone* would highlight the fact that, 'by then, Iron Maiden were superstars of heavy metal', while iTunes would conclude years later that, 'for heavy metal purists', *Powerslave* is an album for which 'there is no substitute'.

Settling on to their throne as the kings of British heavy metal, the band found that the mid-1980s were a relatively peaceful period, personally and professionally. As Bruce Dickinson recalled candidly to *Kerrang!* 'There was much more friction between 1981 and 1983 than there ever was afterwards! We nearly came to blows on the *Number of the Beast* tour. In fact, Steve wanted to fuckin' sack me after two weeks but Rod [Smallwood, Maiden manager] said he had to live with me!

'Steve isn't a guy who naturally likes change. He's conservative with a small "c" – very quiet and reserved offstage. He's very determined about keeping control of Maiden and maintaining its direction. All that early tension between us actually fuelled the band! So this calmer period was also a very productive one for Iron Maiden.'

So this calmer period was also a very productive one for Iron Maiden. Before flying to Compass Point again to track the new album with producer Martin Birch, the band's songwriting would flourish into new territory that *Billboard* would conclude 'catalogues every major facet of the band's personality during the Dickinson years and does so while firing on all cylinders. Perhaps that's in part because *Powerslave* is the first Maiden album to feature the same line-up as its predecessor, creating a definite continuity and comfort level. Or perhaps it's simply that we're witnessing a great band in its creative prime.'

Or as iTunes would later note, the band, 'having firmly established themselves as true heavy-metal warriors', used 'their esteemed status in the metal community to further indulge their musical complexities'.

Pulling the creative curtain back on the band's songwriting process after five years together, Steve Harris told journalist Johnny B, 'Normally we just go in and do it, and rehearse the songs in the studio, and we would allocate ourselves a specific period of time before that when we write the songs ... Sometimes we just pair up or sometimes it was whoever was around at the time. Sometimes it was whoever was available for writing. Sometimes you think you might want to take a song in a certain direction with one person or another. Sometimes it's not even like that, it's whoever is up for doing stuff at that particular time you are working on that particular song. There's no big deal about it.'

Drummer Nicko McBrain added years later in a conversation with MetalSludge.com that Harris, at times, even indulged his hobbies for inspiration when working on the band's new studio material. 'Steve loves to play soccer and be with his family but, when he gets into Maiden mode, he's like totally possessed and driven to that end. He's got a real active mind, which, in turn, gives him the majority of the ideas that he comes up with.'

The band's collective creative energies would produce multiple hits, fan favourites and live staples for years to come. These included 'Two Minutes to Midnight', which would rise to No. 11 in the UK singles chart and No. 25 in *Billboard*'s Top Album Tracks on its release as a single. The song inspired *Billboard* to say it captured Maiden 'at its catchiest', while the BBC concluded the song was an 'early highlight' of the album, honing in on how the 'opening drum damage dives into a finger-itching bassline and infectious hi-hat, over the top of a brilliantly energetic riff that's perfectly complemented by Dickinson's galloping-horse vocal delivery. It's an example of hard-rock perfection.'

Looking back, guitarist Adrian Smith said of the song's composition, 'I could knock out stuff like that all day but it didn't always fit into the kind of fantasy-horror thing that Maiden had going for them. In the early days I needed Bruce to help me make things more how Maiden would want them. "Two Minutes to Midnight" is a perfect example of that. I had the right riff and Bruce had the right words.'

Dickinson, in the same conversation with Ironmaiden.com, would say of writing the song 'Powerslave' that it was 'more than just about the ancient Egyptians; it was also about us, the band, and what was happening to us. We were slaves to the power, whether musically or in terms of just chasing success. We were both.'

Reflecting in the band's official biography on what the band achieved in writing and recording *Powerslave*, Steve Harris would tell biographer Mick Wall that, years after its original release, the album remained one of his favourites from the band's growing catalogue. 'I still think it's a really, really strong album. I think there are four stand-out tracks on there, all of which we did live, and [they are] "Rime of the Ancient Mariner", "Two Minutes to Midnight", "Powerslave" and "Aces High". Of the other tracks on there ... there are some good ones. There's "The Duelists", which I still think is really good ... it's musically interesting. But if you put [it] against "Rime of the Ancient Mariner" and "Two Minutes to Midnight", it's just no way. But they weren't filler songs or anything like that. I just think those four particular songs were really strong.'

Released on 2 September 1984, the album reached No. 2 on the UK albums chart, while in the US *Powerslave* went to No. 21 on the *Billboard* 200 Album Chart and remained in the Top 25 of the magazine's dominant album chart.

Critics were as in love with the album as fans, with *Billboard* saying, 'If *The Number of the Beast* was the all-time metal landmark, *Powerslave* is perhaps the quintessential Maiden album, capturing all the signature elements of the band's definitive era in one place ... *Powerslave* summarises why Iron Maiden was so important and influential even more effectively than *The Number of the Beast*, at least on a purely musical level ... It's every bit as classic and essential.'

Following the release of *Powerslave* the band embarked on a year-long worldwide tour that covered 26 countries and resulted in the subsequent release of the band's first live LP, 1985's *Live After Death* – widely regarded as one of the best live heavy-metal albums of all time.

Released at a time when live albums had become as much a staple of any rock or metal band's catalogue – from Ozzy Osbourne's *Tribute* to Kiss's *ALIVE* series – Iron Maiden's *Live After Death* was no exception to that series of greatness in live recording.

In recording *Live After Death*, Harris would explain to biographer Mick Wall that 'we wanted to do a proper live album 'cause that's what we've always been about, playing live. I think we've always had the problem in the studio – still do to a certain extent, I suppose – of trying to recreate what we do live. When you listen to a live version of one of our songs, nine times out of ten it's much better than the original recorded version. It's very difficult to create the same atmosphere when you go into the studio. We used to joke that we should get a load of cardboard cut-outs of a crowd and put them in there to make us think we're doing a gig, just to get us in the right vibe.'

Billboard's review best sums up *Live After Death*. Along with most of its critical peers, the magazine considered it a masterpiece, the sum of the many parts that made up Iron's Maiden's World Slavery Tour. 'One of the longest and most extensive tours ever undertaken by a rock band, [it lasted] from 9 August 1984 to 5 July 1985 and visited such countries as Poland, Austria, Hungry, Yugoslavia, Italy, France, Spain, Portugal, Scotland, England, Germany, Sweden, Canada, Japan and the US. The show itself included a mammoth set-up that replicated the intricate ancient Egyptian scenery of the *Powerslave* album cover.

'As a thank you to the hundreds of thousands of fans who packed arenas the world over, the double-disc live set *Live After Death* was issued in 1985. Disc one comprised selections from a four-night stand at LA's Long Beach Arena, while disc two consisted of performances from London's Hammersmith Odeon. The album is essentially a best-of of sorts, since most of their singles released up to this point are featured in all of their high-decibel glory: "Aces High", "Two Minutes to Midnight", "The Trooper", "Flight of Icarus", "The Number of the Beast", "Run to the Hills" and

"Running Free". Also included are such strong album tracks as "Wrathchild", "22 Acacia Avenue", "Children of the Damned", "Phantom of the Opera", "Hallowed Be Thy Name" and "Iron Maiden", plus the two epics "Powerslave" and "Rime of the Ancient Mariner", making it a near-complete overview. *Live After Death* is easily one of heavy metal's best live albums.'

CHAPTER SIX

SOMEWHERE IN TIME (1986)

'I went off into acoustic world and I wanted to do almost like an unplugged record for the next Iron Maiden album, except this was years before MTV started doing it.'
Bruce Dickinson

Somewhere in Time was the band's sixth album and the second in what the *Guardian* would hail as 'a great trio of albums' that began with *Powerslave*, and would wind up with *Seventh Son of a Seventh Son.* As Steve Harris recalled to KNAC years later, it found the band working under a great deal of pressure, 'coming off one tour and having a week off and going straight into writing the next album and rehearsing, and then going straight out into the next world tour. And we did that for the first four or five albums.'

That pace resulted in the notable absence of Bruce Dickinson from any of the album's writing credits, which Harris said was attributable, in part, to the fact that 'Bruce was so fried he couldn't even write anything, really. Anything coherent, anyway ... Without a doubt, he was the one affected the most ... I can't imagine what it's like singing the way he does every night. It's just incredibly taxing on him ...

He's got fantastic pipes but to go out and ask him to do that every night for six nights a week for two hours a night for thirteen months is a lot to ask of anybody.'

Dickinson agreed, at least in part, conceding to the band's biographer Mick Wall that after the *Powerslave* tour 'we were supposed to have six months off, which quickly became four months. I was just sitting around and gradually started to come back to some sort of sense that, well, "OK, as long as we're not doing any more of these crazy tours, you know, let's see how we go." Because, to me, the touring thing just wasn't enough. Going out and playing in front of ten thousand people – OK, great, but that's not what I got into music for, exclusively. I got into the music business because I wanted to tell stories and I wanted to explore the inside of my head and communicate it to people, and I thought, "Well, what would really give me a buzz, to go off and do another twelve-month tour would be if we had another fucking record that I really felt was ground breaking."'

For Dickinson, that translated to a stylistic departure, opting for a decidedly acoustic direction – the opposite of anything remotely resembling what his bandmates had in mind for *Somewhere in Time*. 'If it had been my way, the album would have sounded very different,' he said, adding that '*Powerslave*, for me, felt like sort of natural rounding off of *Piece of Mind* and *The Number of the Beast*, that whole sort of era. I remember listening back to it and I thought, "Ummm, this is great but I don't know how much more we can do of records that sound in this kind of vein." I felt we had to come up with our *Physical Graffiti* or our *Led*

Zeppelin IV, or whatever, that we had to get it on to another level or we'd stagnate and just drift away.

'It wasn't so much that it had to be acoustic; I just felt that we should be leading and not following. I felt that we were right there, at that point, that we had the whole world literally at our feet, waiting for what we were gonna come up with next. And I felt that, if we came up with the same old thing, people would accept it and people would buy it but, if it was me, there'd be a tiny bit of disappointment there too ... I just thought the time was right for us to do something audacious, something vast and daring, and I didn't feel that we did that with *Somewhere in Time*. We just made another Iron Maiden album.'

Naturally the singer's bandmates viewed the situation differently. Steve Harris's matter-of-fact opinion, shared with Wall, was that 'Bruce just wasn't himself at that time ... I just thought he'd lost the plot completely ... We didn't realise at first but he was probably more burned out than anyone at the end of the last tour. Then, when we came back to do the next album, he just couldn't seem to get himself together with any of the writing or anything. He came in with a few ideas, which didn't really suit. It wasn't 'cause it was acoustic, necessarily, or even that it was very different sort of stuff; it was just that we didn't think it was good enough, really.'

Conceding years later that he 'could see he would feel bad that his songs were rejected,' Harris still reasoned that the band was none the wiser because 'he seemed to accept it quite readily at the time 'cause he realised that he was ... not on a different planet but he was sort of edging that way. He knew he was feeling a bit strange so he just let us get on with it and, luckily enough, Adrian came in with some strong stuff on his own and that was that.'

Picking up the creative slack, Smith contributed mightily to the writing of *Somewhere in Time*, particularly where hits were concerned. The guitarist shared a bit about his writing process for the album with IronMaiden.com. 'I always put ideas down on tape,' he said, 'then, when the time comes, it's just a matter of adjusting them. I make rough demos.' Offering 'Wasted Years', one of the biggest hits off of *Somewhere in Time* as an example, he said, 'I got the idea from messing around with a guitar synthesiser.'

Once Smith had the words and full music completed Steve Harris quipped to *Metal Hammer* that 'Adrian was afraid to let me hear "Wasted Years" because he thought that it was too different ... Adrian definitely had a commercial edge, "Wasted Years" being an example of that,' adding that, in his opinion, at the end of the day, 'a good song is a good song, no matter what it sounds like'.

Elaborating on his writing for the album, Smith recalled to Mick Wall that 'We'd had a little lay-off and Bruce just wasn't around for a while, and I think he had pretty definite ideas about what he wanted to write next anyway. So I was just sort of left to my own devices and the songs just came with the words already there.'

Harris, the album's other main writer, told journalist Johnny B about his own writing process. 'Nine times out ten we will already have a melody, a really strong melody, and we will write the lyrics to the melody. That's how we do things usually. So then we are trying to fit a lyric to a melody that may have already created a mood. You then have to write something that will suit that – you can't really write something that won't suit that song. That is where, lyrically, I get my inspiration from, the vibe and the mood of the song.'

As the band approached the start of recording, amazingly, no one had yet broken the news to Bruce Dickinson that the acoustic songs he'd submitted for the album had been voted down by the band. In the end it was producer Martin Birch who wound up as the messenger, as Dickinson recalled to Mick Wall. The bombshell was dropped 'in the Bahamas when we were recording the album and Martin told me that the others didn't like my songs. So I went away and thought, "Well, what shall I do here? Shall I throw a wobbler, pack my toys and go home?" But I'd gotten far enough away from the state of mind I was at, at the end of the *Powerslave* tour, to go, "Well, who knows? They could be right. Maybe I am a basket case." And so I convinced myself I should go with it. In a way I felt like I was just unburdening myself of responsibility.' Still, in hindsight, Dickinson admitted, 'I felt very much like a fly being swatted. [It] left me quashed for a long time inside.'

For his part, Birch agreed with the band and candidly offered Wall his own reasoning on why the material was rejected. 'I always sensed a slight danger of too much input from Bruce and Adrian because they were always in danger of kind of taking it away from what Maiden really was.

Some of their songs just weren't suitable – like a Bryan Adams-type thing that Adrian came up with called 'Reach Out', this sort of US stadium rock one as a B-side. But to have let the band put something like that on the album would have taken away from the whole point of Iron Maiden. Neither Steve nor I ever envisaged the band as anything other than what they were.

'The other songs Adrian wrote for the album – like 'Wasted Years' – they were great but even they walked the line a little bit, I felt. As for Bruce's songs, they were all acoustic and they just didn't fit. They had to go. Not because they were acoustic but because they just weren't right. But we didn't make a big deal about it. Bruce has written some great songs for Maiden and we knew he'd write more. These ones just weren't right.'

Years later Dickinson would tell Maidenfans.com, 'The more I look at it now, the more it was like a conscious reaction – like your brain throwing a temper tantrum, saying, 'I'm not going to write any more of this stuff! I hate it! Look what it's done to me! Why can't I stick my finger in my ear and go and be a folkie, and drink beer like everybody else?' I was very messed-up in the brain department at the time.

'I was talking to Steve about it and even he had a lot of head problems after the *Powerslave* tour, and nobody had really resolved them by the time we came to do *Somewhere in Time*. I think I came to terms with it more after we'd done the album. We had quite a long gap, and then went out and did the tour, which still ended up being two months longer than it was supposed to be, of course!'

One departure the band did make with their sound was the heavier infusion of keyboards into the mix. As iTunes put it, following 'such superb albums as *The Number of the Beast*, *Piece of Mind* and *Powerslave*, Iron Maiden had forged a completely original heavy-metal sound. Feeling that they'd taken it as far it could go, the band decided to broaden their sound with the use of synthesisers for their sixth studio album, 1986's *Somewhere in Time*. While many other metal bands used synths in the 1980s to appeal to the pop audience, Maiden wisely did not overindulge. Instead, they used them to create textures and were rewarded with one of their most commercially successful releases.'

In spite of the welcoming reception by the band's fan base, Harris recalled years later in an interview with Ironmaiden.com that, at the time, 'We took horrendous flak from some quarters for introducing guitar synths. In fact, with nearly every album we've done someone somewhere has had a pop at us for doing something wrong. That's not my paranoia either and, if anything, that winds me up to prove everyone wrong. If it pisses me off enough, it gives me a real edge.'

Years later in a conversation with *Metal Hammer* Harris added his feeling that the band perhaps deserved more credit for the boundaries they'd successfully pushed with their sound as it had evolved from album to album. 'For years we've tried out lots of different things and we always take flak for it. We took stick when we first did "Flight of Icarus", which was different for us, and then again for "Wasted Years" (a 1986 song, which featured guitar synths). I say it in every interview I do but it's true: all we're trying to do is get the best collection of songs that we can.'

Offering fans an inside look into how the synthesisers were tracked during recording, Michael Kinney, the band's keyboards man (and Steve's longtime bass tech), told *Keyboard* magazine, 'As a player, Maiden was my first – and only – big-league recording situation. Steve Harris pretty much knows what he wants so it was just my job to play it. I played on a few albums (*No Prayer for the Dying*, *Fear of the Dark*, *X Factor* and some of *Virtual XI*). Around then Steve started feeling more comfortable with keys and began doing most of it. On *Somewhere in Time* they started using guitar and bass synths, and I helped with programming ... They used keyboard synths and studio toys. Steve comes up with a bit every now and then, and a lot of the synth parts are reinforcing things that Adrian used synth guitar on.'

Guitarist Smith added his recollection in an interview with IronMaiden.com that, 'I used one of the first Roland guitar synths on the album. I think techonology's great as long as you don't lose the vibe.'

Remembering a chaotic recording schedule once tracking was underway, Steve Harris told Wall, 'We went a bit crazy. We recorded the bass and drums down in Nassau, at Compass Point, then went to Holland – to Wisseloord Studios, in Hilversum – to do the guitars and vocals, and then Martin took it back to New York to mix it at Electric Ladyland Studios. It was crazy but we were just desperately trying to get it right without hurrying it for a change and, well, you learn from your mistakes, I suppose.'

In spite of his lack of involvement in writing the album, Dickinson's voice was as relevant as ever to the magic Maiden produced in the studio. As *Billboard* would later note in its review of the record, 'You also can't discuss Maiden without touching on Dickinson's voice. The vocal equivalent of smoking freshly smelted Sheffield steel, sweating, soaring, clad in leather and studs, it's a combination of gifted genetics, operatic chutzpah and gallons of Newcastle Brown Ale ... Dickinson's vocal dexterity and ability to lift songs that could sound ordinary if they weren't delivered with such bravado and abandon.'

Released on 29 September 1986, *Somewhere in Time* shot to No. 3 on the UK album chart and No. 11 on *Billboard*'s Top 200 Album Chart, driven, in part, by the success of the singles 'Wasted Years' and 'Stranger in a Strange Land'.

The BBC's summary of the LP would highlight the fact that 'this new collection of Iron Maiden tracks contains work from a period that was creatively their busiest and, arguably, most successful ... It's straight-ahead, grab-some-furniture, shake-your-brain-for-three-and-a-half-minutes (stopping when you get a bit dizzy, or to have a swig of snakebite) rock. This collection is a fascinating reflection of the extent to which Iron Maiden defined heavy metal's enduring themes and styles: alienation, allegory, fantasy, the occult, exploitation and abuse of power. They're also pioneers in terms of understanding that this music is theatre: not just something to be played but really performed.'

In 2010 iTunes would conclude that, ultimately, *Somewhere in Time*'s greatest success was in 'broadening

Maiden's sound without alienating their longtime metal fans'. Years after its original release, it is still a critical and fan favourite.

CHAPTER SEVEN

SEVENTH SON OF A SEVENTH SON (1988)

'*Seventh Son of a Seventh Son* pushed the sound in a progressive direction'
Antimusic.com

'I remember having to justify ourselves with the *Seventh Son of a Seventh Son* album because we'd used guitars synthesisers' Steve Harris

'The relationship between me and Steve gets better and stronger with every album'
Bruce Dickinson

Concept albums are brave territory for any artist, especially in the late-1980s metal scene. As *Billboard* noted, this was a time when 'harsh thrash metal and radio-friendly glam rock were the two chief heavy-metal styles. Instead of aligning themselves to either camp, Iron Maiden stuck to their guns and issued a concept album, *Seventh Son of a Seventh Son*.' Though they didn't break any remarkable new ground stylistically with the release, the band reinforced their position as the most cutting-edge concept-metal band in the business with their newest studio LP at a time when every band from Queensryche to Metallica to Megadeth were all following the trend.

From chief songwriter Steve Harris's perspective, however, little had changed creating their latest record. 'We just try and write the best songs that we can,' he told rock journalist Johnny B, 'and we try and be natural to the way we are feeling at that time.' Of the aforementioned musical trends he added, 'At the end of the day you can't worry about that sort of thing – you just have to concentrate on writing the best song that you can. Actually, it is fair to say that, if we feel something is too similar to something we have done before, we bin it – honest! We don't like repeating ourselves but it has to be right and we have to feel right with it. It is the most important thing.'

This time the band chose Musicland Studios in Munich, Germany as their ground zero between late 1987 and March 1988. Built by legendary Italian record producer Giorgio Moroder in the late 1960s, it housed over the following 20 years such rock legends as Marc Bolan & T.Rex, Led Zeppelin, Electric Light Orchestra, the Rolling Stones, Sparks, Queen, Deep Purple, Sweet and Elton John, among many others.

According to TheHistoryofRock.com, the sound of those records and their collective success created 'the so-called Munich Sound' although, as [Moroder's fellow writer-producer] Pete Bellotte pointed out, there was nothing particularly German about it. Rather, it was a meeting point for talent drawn from all parts of Europe. Say Yes Productions, run by Bellotte (English) and Moroder (Italian), employed an Icelandic arranger and a team of session players (who recorded a couple of albums as the

Munich Machine), drawn largely from Britain and other parts of Europe.'

Indeed, Moroder himself was modest about the technical layout. 'Our studios here at Musicland are just typical. Nearly all the equipment there is standard, English or American.'

From a writing perspective, Steve Harris recalled to Johnny B that, when deciding to do a concept album, 'we had sat down and talked about that beforehand. The main reason, it was agreed, was because it was a really strong idea. Whereas a lot of people thought that quite a few of the albums were concept albums because they had strong imagery and a strong link between some of the songs ... We don't tend to analyse too much of what we are doing – we just write ... the best songs we can, and then we try and get the best imagery, etc. that we can to go with them.'

Bruce Dickinson told journalist Sylvie Simmons of the songwriting for *Seventh Son of a Seventh Son*, 'Instead of looking at it like Lego bricks – this bit goes here and that bit goes there – it was just getting the feeling right that made it work. Whereas before I think we tended to plan everything out a lot, on the new album we sort of loosened up a bit and that made all the difference. There's a lot more experimentation. I think we've broken the mould a bit. With all the previous albums you can say, "Well, this is a bit better than that one," or, "That was a bit like that one." They all refer back to one another. But this – although it's obviously Iron Maiden – it's quite distinctly different from anything we've ever done before.'

In part, because of the band's creative chemistry, producer Martin Birch told *Best* magazine that camaraderie was key to successfully pulling off records as ambitious as Maiden did consistently. 'The fact that we know each other much better now has improved the quality of our collaboration. The fact that I'm used to the bands I have worked with helps me to know instantly what they want or even what they can achieve.' In fact, he added, Iron Maiden was 'my favourite band to work with ... the producer/band relationship is much more constructive.'

Before the band went to Germany, Dickinson recalled in an interview with Sylvie Simmons, 'We wrote the album round Steve's house in Essex in his old barn, which sounds great, a good atmosphere to work in. And Adrian came around my house a couple of times, and then we all went into the studio. We gave ourselves a starting point. We all guaranteed that we would not bother each other until this point and then after that it was really a free-for-all. It's nothing personal, nothing to do with not liking each other – it's all to do with the general situation.

'As you grow older you realise that rock music is not actually the real world. Being on the road and all the rest of it is only a part of your life and, with any luck, most of your life is going to be lived outside of tour buses and inside theatres. And you either have to come to terms with that or become a casualty of some description. What we're tending to do now is try and get the real life and the rock life to co-exist. Steve's going to have Lorraine, his two kids and his nanny in a complete tour bus of his own when he goes to tour in America, and Nicko's going to be flying his own aircraft around, that sort of thing.'

Reflecting on a commitment to bringing their latest studio experience as fully to life for fans live as possible, Dickinson spoke candidly about the challenges of touring as expansively as the band did. 'With this tour we've said we'll keep it to six months, make it in the summer to avoid getting flu and being miserable, and killing yourself, and just go out and have a good time. When it's got a starting point and an ending point, I can plan my life around that. I know what time I've got to relax in and when my life is not really my own – because that's what it really amounts to. You're giving up your freedom to drop everything and commit yourself a hundred per cent.'

Discussing what the *Chicago Tribune* highlighted as the 'compositional fluidity' of *Seventh Son of a Seventh Son*, Dickinson offered the first single, 'Can I Play with Madness', as a successful example of 'a real collaborative effort. The beginning bit, the riff – with apologies to Pete Townshend! – was me on acoustic guitar at home. Then Adrian came along with some chords and I went, "Hang on a minute – I've got some words here that fit," so we sat around and worked on it. And I said, "Can I write an instrumental bit in the middle?" – because I normally don't write bits like that since I don't have to play them – and Steve came in with the time-change bit, the Zeppelin-y bit. We had a tremendous argument, with Nicko saying, "Oh, it won't work – it's too radical." And I thought, "No, it will work, so long as everyone takes the plunge and does it."'

As rock journalist Ian Fortnam noted of the finished album, '*Seventh Son* finds Iron Maiden at their most assured and creative. Essentially, this is a spectacular example of 22-carat heavy metal,' while I-tunes thought the album found Maiden 'at their proggiest, with abrupt, stop-on-a-dime transitions between riffs, tempos, time signatures, and song sections ... [and] every song has a memorable chorus.'

Detailing some of how that result worked from a guitarist's perspective, newcomer Janick Gers – who would take over from Adrian Smith in 1990 – told Metal-Rules.com, 'There are a lot of guitars that are overdubbed. A lot of higher octaves, lower octaves, harmonies sometimes, even three-part harmonies. Sometimes harmonies where there is a guitar underlying everything and when you play live, you have to decide which ones you are going to use and which ones you are not going to use, and sometimes you have to leave quite a bit out.'

In terms of crafting the album's broader soundscape, Bruce Dickinson told Simmons, 'We didn't get a keyboard player for the album. It's mainly one-finger stuff from Adrian, Steve, the engineer or whoever had a finger free at the time. Some parts of the album are much sparser than other things we've done, and there's a lot of depth and complexity at times but it still sounds a lot clearer. Before, sometimes we tended to have a bit of a wall-of-sound and you had to listen quite hard to get through to what individual layers were doing. But it's very transparent, the solos really leap out of the speakers and you can hear everything.'

Steve Harris added that the album was particularly fun for

him personally to create because 'I'm really influenced by big, epic film-theme music. I love that type of music.'

Dickinson offered 'Infinite Dreams' as an example of the band's more experimental side on the album, describing an opening that 'starts out really dreamy and Hendrix-y, and has all kinds of things all over it, and the whole thing just builds up. And there's also a lot of uptempo stuff, that certain kind of feel that Maiden's got anyway, where people will say, "Yeah! Back into the groove!" sort of thing.'

Becoming their first No. 1 album since *The Number of the Beast* six years earlier, *Seventh Son of a Seventh Son* became an instant classic for the band – so much so that years later the millennium generation of music critics were as in love with it as their print-media predecessors had been. *Rock Band* hailed the album as 'amazing' while iTunes' thought the LP 'ranks among their best work'.

On its release on 11 April 1988, *Seventh Son of a Seventh Son* went to No. 1 in the UK album chart and No. 12 on *Billboard*'s Top 200 Album Chart. It also produced a staggering four hit singles – 'Can I Play With Madness', 'The Evil That Men Do', 'The Clairvoyant (Live)' and 'Infinite Dreams (Live)', which reached Nos 3, 5, 6 and 6, respectively, in the UK.

For singer Bruce Dickinson, the results he and his ever-ambitious band mates achieved were 'as different from the last album as *The Number of the Beast* was from *Killers*. About the closest you could get to it is probably *Piece of Mind* but it's very different from that too, much more up front.'

Steve Harris added in a conversation with a European rock journalist that fans were 'a bit freaked out' by the production 'but that's what we wanted at the time and I still stand by that ... As an actual sounding album it didn't sound at all like the others.'

Seventh Son of a Seventh Son would also mark the band's last collaboration – as it seemed at the time – with Adrian Smith, who left the band in 1990. The band decided to carry on as a two-some where axes were concerned, feeling Smith's presence was one they couldn't fully replace with anyone else. Smith's departure came as a shock to the group and Bruce Dickinson admitted years later to a rock journalist, 'I think everybody was a bit surprised at how much we missed him and certainly I don't think anybody had realised how much the fans would miss him – big time.'

CHAPTER EIGHT

NO PRAYER FOR THE DYING (1990)

'I am open to different-sounding stuff ... if it's any good'
Steve Harris

The cryptically titled *No Prayer for the Dying* introduced new guitarist Janick Gers, who had played in Ian Gillan's solo band and on Dickinson's solo album *Tattooed Millionaire*. It was during the recording of that project that he was asked to replace the departing Adrian Smith.

Working once again with long-time producer Martin Birch, the band recorded at Barnyard Studios on Steve Harris's farm in Essex between June and September 1990. 'To me, *No Prayer For The Dying* was really like a live album done in the studio,' Harris would explain to a European rock journalist. 'If we had stuck audience noise on it, most people would have thought it was a live album. Because that's the way we approached it, very raw, very fresh, did it real quick. That was the approach we wanted at the time.'

Bruce Dickinson added more detail to *Classic Rock*

magazine. '*No Prayer* was actually recorded using a antiquated, knackered recording truck – the Rolling Stones mobile – that needed a good refurbishment ... It was recorded in a barn, in winter with the mobile outside ... and it was shit. It was a shit-sounding record and I wish we hadn't done it that way. At the time I was as guilty as anyone else in going, "Oh great! Look, we are all covered in straw. What a larf!"'

By this point Iron Maiden had their craft down to a science. For Harris and Dickinson, the group's two primary songwriting forces, the individual creative process varied. For Dickinson, music wasn't the only thing going on in his life, as he explained in an interview with *Kerrang!* 'I write whenever I've got a chunk of time and I don't have to do anything else. I like to clear the decks and concentrate for a while. I always have a guitar downstairs to doodle on and maybe write a few tunes with it ... Anyway that's how I usually spend my day. I nip in and out. One thing that takes up my time is starting a small company to import fencing equipment from China and selling it here. I've bought a calculator – my first one! It's always better to have too much to do. And there are still loads of things I wanna do.'

Harris, meanwhile, told rock journalist Johnny B, 'We always believe that a song is a short story and then you pick something from within the lyric that describes the song. Lyrics are important ... though not the most important thing. I would say the music and the melodies of the vocal lines are the most important. However, having said that, the lyrics shouldn't just be a load of old crap. That is why we have always tried to make them mean something so people can read into them whatever they want. Having said that though, they still need to mean something to us and that's why the melody lines have to be really, really strong.

'This is a question that we've been asked before because sometimes, just sometimes, you do land up compromising slightly with lyrics if you have a specific strong melody and there are some words you wanna use. I have had it before where you can't use what you want to use. For example, I write to the syllable ... So if there is a particular word I want to use which doesn't fit because it might have three syllables instead of two ... I then have to go and find another word, which means the same thing, with two syllables. That's when it becomes difficult because you can't always find the word which means exactly what you want to say. It does become a problem sometimes.

'It's not just like writing some poetry. When you are writing to a melody, it has got to fit. If you then compromise the melody, that's not always on because, if it is such a strong melody, it's very important to keep that melody intact. That should have sent people to sleep!'

Elaborating on the inspiration behind some of the specific songs on the album, Dickinson began with the racy 'Tailgunner', whose title he revealed to *Classic Rock* came from 'a porno movie about anal sex'. 'Then I thought, "Well, I can't write the lyrics about that!" So I wrote it about real tailgunners. I had some words, which began, "Trace your way back fifty years, to the glow of Dresden, blood and tears." I know we shouldn't mention the war but it's about the attitude of bombing people. It was real death in the skies back then. But there aren't any tailgunners on planes any more – it's all done by computers, using missiles. At least it used to be man on man but now it's machine on machine. Who uses bullets any more?'

Moving on to 'Fate's Warning', a tune the BBC hailed as 'episodic prog rock', Dickinson recalled that the song began with 'Steve's words again. This is about feeling secure when everyone's life can hang by a thread. You can go any time and who knows why or how?'

Targeting the censorship-happy, morally driven yet hypocritical religious right, the singer recalled of 'Holy Smoke' – which the BBC called 'meat and grist to rock bands of all shades and sizes' – that the lyrics were an indictment of 'TV preachers and all the various lies they tell. I just had this big image of all those ovens in the death camps with the preachers' feet sticking out and holy smoke going up.'

Adding to their list of targets, the band centered in on 'green hypocrites' with the comically titled 'Public Enema Number One'. 'It's about a big guy with his fast car and he's leaving the city in a cloud of smoke, leaving the children crying in fear,' the singer explained. 'He's got a one-way ticket out of here. Fine, see ya. Because he can afford it he's left everyone else behind and in the cities there is overcrowding, guns and riots, and it seems like everything is gonna snap. The politicians just lie to save their own skins, gamble that they are gonna do the right thing, and they give the press scapegoats all the time. The whole thing is based on a cross between New York and LA, and I just hope the kids of today have more brains than the frazzled remains of the 1960s and the 1970s generations ... "California dreaming as the Earth dies screaming" – that's what it's about. People talking about the environment and not doing anything.'

Banned by the BBC even though it shot to No. 1 on the UK singles chart, 'Bring Your Daughter... to the Slaughter' was the band's biggest hit off the album. 'Here I tried to sum up what I thought *Nightmare on Elm Street* movies are really about and it's all about adolescent fear of period pains,' the singer said. 'That's what I think it is – deep down. When a young girl first gets her period, she bleeds and it happens at night, and so she is afraid to go to sleep and it's a very terrifying time for her, sexually as well, and *Nightmare on Elm Street* targets that fear. The real slaughter in the Freddie movies is when she loses her virginity. That is the rather nasty thought behind it all but that's what makes those kinds of movies frightening.'

Delving deeper into the dark side of the band's lyrical landscape, Dickinson said of 'The Assassin', 'Here we are trying to get into the head of a hired killer. He doesn't do it for money but because he likes it and he's cool, calculating, cold and sadistic. These are Steve's lyrics again.'

Taking on the Soviets – like every other metal band in the late 1980s and early 1990s – with 'Mother Russia', Iron Maiden, as Dickinson saw it, were focusing on 'the tragedy of a great land, which has an incredible history of being overrun and people being massacred, for centuries, and this song says: wouldn't it be great if Russia could finally get itself together now and live in peace?' BBC would hail the result as an 'epic album closer'.

Expanding further on the topic of war, Dickinson identified 'Dive, Dive, Dive' as arising 'from one of my favourite war movies. We do use a lot of film and book titles because they always inspire good material for us. But then books crop up a lot in films! This is about the dog-eat-dog, no-mercy world of life and death at sea during the Second World War, and it was as rough for the guys below as it was for the guys up top. They both engaged in this evil struggle without any mercy. And the sea didn't have any mercy.'

Indulging their provocative side on 'Hooks in You', Dickinson explained that the song was 'a slightly tongue-in-cheek thing. Me and Paddy went to look at a house to buy, and it was lived in by three gay guys. We looked around and it had all these beams, and one of the guys was obviously into S&M and leather and stuff, and in one room there were these enormous industrial hooks screwed into the beams. My mind boggled at what they could be used for. I went home and wrote "Hooks in You" with the line "All the hooks in the ceiling, that well-hung feeling."

'I couldn't write it about gay guys but what if you went round to the house of Mr and Mrs Average [and] you found all these hooks in the ceiling? What do *they* get up to? At the end of the song the guy thinks his wife has been unfaithful and sets her in concrete in the foundations.'

Singling out the title track 'No Prayer for the Dying' as 'one of the best quiet-beginning-type songs I've ever done with Maiden', Dickinson said, 'This song has Steve's lyrics and, for me, it has the best vocals on the album – the one I like best, even though it's like just two lines ... and I really like the melody line.'

In its review of *No Prayer for the Dying* the BBC concluded that the band had achieved 'a tight formation of terse bass lines, sprightly solos, hooks and last-minute precision twists that veer clear away off to the left field just when you think it's about to collide head on with a HM cliché.' iTunes celebrated the release as 'an impressive CD that has its share of assets. Bruce Dickinson is consistently spirited and the writing is undeniably solid on such gothic scorchers as "Fate's Warning", "Tailgunner" and "Run Silent, Run Deep".'

On the whole, however, critics decided that, although it wasn't their favourite Maiden album, it worked – in the BBC's words – 'most part thanks to bassist Steve Harris's writing. Though overall *No Prayer for the Dying* lacks the consistency of some of their earlier albums, there are more than a few worthwhile detours.'

Reflecting back a few years later, Steve Harris tended to agree, telling a European rock journalist, 'I wouldn't say *No Prayer* is our strongest album but then again I wouldn't say it's our weakest either.' What the album garnered, regardless of any critic or band member's opinion, was a resounding applause from fans who excitedly bought the album up upon release to a double-platinum tune that had become the band's standard sales mark by that point in their decade-plus career as one of the genre's leading metal mainstays.

On release in October 1990 *No Prayer for the Dying* – according to *Billboard* – 'quickly shot up the charts all over the world', including reaching No. 2 on the UK album chart and in the Top 20 of the *Billboard* Top 200 Album Chart in the US. As the 1990s dawned and the hair-metal scene gave way to the rise of grunge, Iron Maiden would soldier on, more popular than ever heading into 1992 and *Fear of the Dark*.

CHAPTER NINE

FEAR OF THE DARK (1992)

'*Fear of the Dark*, to me, was more of a follow-on from Seventh Son' Steve Harris

'A return to form for Iron Maiden' *Billboard*

'*Fear of the Dark* could well be Maiden's most rounded album to date, not only in terms of its diversity but, more significantly, in the songwriting stakes'
Raw magazine

By the time 1992 rolled around many of Iron Maiden's contemporaries were beginning to feel the rust and wear of hair-metal saturation. But Maiden showed no signs of slowing down, moving ahead as the end loomed for metal's 1980s commercial heyday. As the band heading into recording *Fear of the Dark* they seemed to exist in their own category of progressive metal, one that they'd pioneered over 15 years to a level that meant they didn't face the same pressures where retail fan loyalty was concerned. 'I don't think we worry about what's in vogue or what people think of us,' Steve Harris quipped to *Raw* magazine. 'If we did, on this album we'd be like a funk-rap-thrash thing, wouldn't we?'

Deciding the compositional direction of Iron Maiden's music had always been Steve Harris's primary responsibility, along with front man Bruce Dickinson, things wouldn't change with this album.

'I haven't written as much stuff as Steve or Bruce because their songwriting's pretty powerful,' guitarist Dave Murray said, adding that he was comfortable with the arrangement. 'Ever since I joined Maiden in 1976 I've just had this huge springboard that Steve's songwriting has given me to do what I want as far as guitar playing is concerned. There's loads of room to expand and I've never had the feeling that I needed to go out and make a jazz-funk album or anything. I love being in this band and playing the way we do allows me total freedom. I've got other stuff that I've written at home but, at the moment, when I get time off, I'd rather spend it with the family than go fiddling around with it. That's not to say that later I won't go doing something with it but I'm happy with the way things are within the band.'

In the same conversation with *Raw* Harris seemed to express his relief at the band's creative assistance. 'I think it's great getting a load of help from all the others. I mean, on the first two albums I wrote nearly all the material and it was the same on the next two. I've always been prolific, I suppose, but really that put me under a lot of pressure and it's really nice now to have all the others contributing a load of stuff that's really good. It's meant that the pressure's relaxed a little and I've been able to concentrate on a few other things too, like a bit of production.'

For Harris, the deciding factor when it came to which songs wound up on the album – regardless of publishing interests or who'd written what – was 'whether it's a good song or not, that's the bottom line. I mean, Nicko's never written stuff before but, if he brought a song along that was good, we'd use it, no problem. Also it depends on how the collaborations between albums work out, 'cause on the last album I wrote a lot of stuff with Bruce but this time I didn't write with him at all. That's purely because he got together with Janick, then I got together with Janick, and by then we had enough. There's no point having fifteen, sixteen songs, 'cause then four of them can't make the album.

'I haven't really got a load of stuff lying around at home that's got me thinking, "Oh, I'm going to have to put this one on a solo album," or whatever. I just don't tend to write songs all the time. I've got tapes with a load of ideas on them but that's about it. I don't think that there's any time for that kind of stuff as far as I'm concerned because I couldn't hold it together. I'm not like Bruce, who can do five things at once – I just concentrate on one because that just keeps me completely occupied. I think, apart from Bruce, it's the same with all of us. There's so much going on in the band and in the songs that we'd all collapse if we did any more!'

No matter how prolific one band member was compared to another, Harris explained that, at the end of the day, 'one thing about Maiden is that we're not one of the bands who sit around writing twenty or thirty songs and then scratch our heads about which ones to put on the record. We take about six weeks to write an album and then we stop. I don't see the point of doing it any other way because, if you give yourself six months, you'll use those six months and need more. We get on with it and, when we've got enough songs, we record the album. It always seems to work for us so I don't see why we should change that.'

Concurring, Dave Murray added that 'I think that there's no point in us spending years making an album because we've always trusted what we felt was spontaneous. Certainly with this album it's almost like it's all become really exciting again because, as individuals, we've just bonded a lot more. The five of us have really got to know each other better, which I suppose is pretty strange when you think about how long we've been going. I think the other thing is that a few people in the band have had a few outside interests so that's meant that they've come back to Maiden feeling really fresh.'

Continuing the ten-year partnership with producer Martin Birch, Steve Harris described to *Raw* a close-knit creative circle, where the producer had become something like 'this psychologist to us!' Birch affirmed the importance of the closeness between artist and producer in making a great album, telling *Best* magazine, 'I certainly think that you can only make the most out of a band if you know it really well, very much in depth.'

Dave Murray added of Birch's role that, in the thick of it all, he remained the band's most loyal cheerleader. 'When you're working in a situation where you're doing overdubs and stuff, you don't really get to see anyone else apart form Martin. He's the one who psyches you up and who tends to keep you in contact with the songs.'

That said, Murray added, 'Steve has always been pretty involved with the production side of things and this time he took on a lot more responsibility, although that wasn't anything to do with the fact that we'd recorded the album round his house!'

Harris felt that 'having the luxury of our own studio meant that we really didn't have any distractions. A lot of people said, "Oh yeah but you'll have all your kids around," and stuff like that but we just got on with it.'

Bruce Dickinson seemed to be the only dissenter from the opinion that Harris's home studio was the optimum environment for recording. Years later, in an interview with *Classic Rock* magazine, he said, 'There were big limitations on that studio, simply because of its physical size, things like that ... We still had the same barn but this time there was a studio upstairs in it. And there was a slight improvement because Martin came in and supervised the sound.'

Delving more frankly into his issues with the recording set-up, the singer added, 'I think some people were a little bit uneasy about the idea of using the studio but nobody really wanted to voice their unease because Martin was like, "No, it'll be fine." And I think Martin was maybe unwilling to voice his unease as well.'

As for the inspiration behind some of the album's specific tracks, Dickinson told Ironmaidencommentary.com that 'Afraid to Shoot Strangers' was written about 'the people that fought in the Gulf War. It's a song about how shitty war is and that it's started by politicians and has to be finished by ordinary people that don't really want to kill anybody.'

Elaborating on the musical evolution of what he referred to as a 'classic track', Dave Murray added that the band actually showed restraint in arranging the song's multi-layered guitar parts. 'There could've been harmony parts all over the place but they just didn't seem right so we took them off. Sometimes that harmony stuff can just sweeten things too much and we felt that, although we'd used keyboards to maybe add textures to songs, we didn't want the song to lose any of that power ... We've used a lot of harmony parts in the past and everyone's got used to that. With this album it wasn't that we tried to move away from that, it was just that they didn't fit.'

Steve Harris added in the same interview that, listening back to it once it was laid down on tape, he was 'really pleased with that song. From my own point of view and out of my own songs, it's definitely one of my favourites. I've always liked progressive stuff anyway. That's why I liked *Seventh Son* because it had that real 1970s progressive influence and this is a continuation of that.'

Released on 11 May 1992, Iron Maiden's ninth studio LP debuted at No. 2 on the UK album chart and achieved Top 10 positions around the world – New Zealand (No. 4), Germany (No. 5), Switzerland (No. 5), Norway (No. 6), Austria (No. 8), Sweden (No. 8), Australia (No. 11), Japan (No. 11), Canada (No. 12) and the US (No. 12). Two singles released off the album were UK hits: 'Be Quick or Be Dead'

(No. 2) and 'From Here to Eternity' (No. 21), with a live version of the title track reaching No. 5.

The band had also attained enough respect among the upper echelon of music critics to be awarded the 1994 Grammy Award for Best Metal Performance with Vocal for 'Fear of the Dark' and moved a reviewer from *Kerrang!* to declare the album's title track as 'in my top three Iron Maiden songs of all time'. That status has endured through to the modern day, with the *Guardian* hailing 'Fear of the Dark' as a 'venerable classic'.

Billboard noted that the album proved Maiden 'could easily hold their own with younger thrash-metal bands', debunking any suggestion that their momentum was slowing down, while iTunes focused on the ballad 'Wasting Love', which it said 'proves to be one of Maiden's better ballads of the 1990s'.

Reflecting on the album shortly following its release, Steve Harris felt the band had delivered business as usual. 'A lot of people have talked about how varied this new album is but we've always had songs on our records that weren't typical,' he told *Raw*. 'Take "To Tame a Land" from *Piece of Mind*. Even as far back as the first album there's been songs like 'Remember Tomorrow" and "Strange World", which haven't been out-and-out metal anyway.'

While the rest of his band members also felt satisfied with their latest studio LP, Bruce Dickinson was the lone hold-out, revealing to *Classic Rock* magazine that, '*Fear...* actually ended up not that bad but, you know, a little bit under par.' That opinion offers an important insight into why, after touring to support the album, he decided to leave the band a decade after becoming their lead singer. In a May 1993 conversation with *Kerrang!* Dickinson confessed that 'Towards the end, there was this little something inside of me, screaming "For God's sake – there must be something different that you can do!" Some nights on the last leg I'd think to myself, "Why does this feel so much like hard work?" You then start to realise that, actually, perhaps you don't want to do this any more.'

In a 1995 interview Steve Harris admitted feeling the timing wasn't a surprise. 'I wasn't shocked that he was going because I suppose for a couple of years I thought he might jump ship anyway. The fact that he seemed to be back into it at *Fear of the Dark*, it was only when we had a six-week break that something happened. I was mixing the live stuff, and we always knew that we'd go back out and release the live stuff at the end of the tour. Three weeks before the second part of the tour he decided to go so we changed our plans and brought out the live albums a lot earlier.'

Hinting that Dickinson's discontent might have begun earlier than the band's most recent LP, Harris added the revelation that 'I felt it was weirder than *Fear of the Dark* because that's when he had his first solo album out. I thought, if he was going to jump ship, it would have been then. And I actually asked him then if he didn't want to be in the band any more, and he said he really did. But I felt on *No Prayer* and the live performances that maybe he wasn't as into it as he had been. On *Fear of the Dark*, funnily enough,

I felt like he was back into it a lot more. But then again, it's all opinions. Get ten punters, and half will say one thing and half another.'

Harris added, 'I was actually the last one to know.' Knowing the news would 'do my head in', the others had held back. 'They didn't want to tell me.' The band's founder shared his feeling at Dickinson's departure as being 'disappointment, sadness and being pissed off – all at once'. In the same conversation with *Kerrang!* he added that, professionally, regardless of any feelings on a personal level, 'If he can't give Maiden a hundred per cent, we don't want him in the band! That's no disrespect or animosity but there's no point in persuading him to come back or anything. In fact, if he backtracked now and said he wanted to stay, we probably wouldn't let him! Personally, I think he's maybe made a mistake, 'cause I don't see why he couldn't do his solo thing and Maiden. But I suppose he wants to do other things too and Maiden are a hard-working band.'

As the full reality of his longtime cohort's departure set in, Harris admitted feeling really rattled. 'What worried me was that I've always felt confident about Maiden. Bruce quitting knocked me for six and I thought maybe the rest of 'em would be looking to me to be a leader. For a week or so I didn't feel like that but now I feel stronger as time goes on.'

The band would need that strength, as predicted by Dickinson himself in the same interview with *Kerrang!* 'It will probably become very much more Steve's baby now and I certainly don't think it'll plummet just because I've gone. Iron Maiden is like an old warhorse. The trooper, the charging, Roy of the Rovers, the straight arrow, the ball at the back of the net … that's what Steve is.'

Harris was less diplomatic in his sentiments towards his former lead singer. In an interview with *Metal Hammer* several years later he stated frankly that 'Bruce left because he didn't want to be part of this any more. He said he felt "musically inhibited". What annoys me to this day is that, when he did leave, he basically went to every magazine in the world and said bad things about Iron Maiden. He cited reasons for leaving that had never been discussed at band meetings and that got to me. Bruce was in the band for nearly twelve years and I don't think we deserved that kind of treatment from him.'

In the end, for Dickinson, it boiled down to the fact that '[I have] found my new musical direction'. Once he'd attained that focus he added *to Kerrang!* 'I [had] to go. I can't stay. *Tattooed Millionaire* was a lot of fun but it wasn't life changing. My new record is changing my life; that's more important than anything.'

CHAPTER TEN

THE X FACTOR (1995)

Changes abounded in 1994 for Iron Maiden. With a new lead singer and a new producer, they opted to christen their new studio LP *The X Factor*, being uncertain how fans would embrace their new front man Blaze Bayley. This weighed heavily on band leader Steve Harris, as he acknowledged in an interview with a European rock journalist ahead of the album's release. 'When you've got a key band-member change – the lead singer – that ... is a big deal ... Obviously with a different person in the band the pressure of this album is so big – new singer, we've been away from it for a while ... The pressure is there.'

One area the band didn't feel any real stress over internally was in welcoming new vocalist Blaze Bayley into the band. As guitarist Dave Murray later recalled to Maidenfans.com, 'When Blaze came and started singing, we knew immediately that he would fit in the band. He came from another hard-rock band so he could suit Maiden perfectly. The same goes for all the other line-up changes. That way there was continuity. An example of the opposite is when Glenn Hughes went into Deep Purple. He came from a different musical direction and that changed the band's identity. That's not always wrong but in Maiden we always wanted musicians who fit in the concept.

In the same interview fellow guitarist Janick Gers added, 'As far as Bruce is concerned, I still don't know why he left us. A few weeks before he told us he was leaving I'd had a chat with him about the band and he thought everything was going all right. When I heard he was leaving us, I was totally surprised.'

Asked what the differences were between the two singers, the guitarist added in the same conversation, 'It's still Iron Maiden. He sings maybe a bit more like Paul Di'Anno did but Paul, Bruce and Blaze show each a side of Maiden ... Bruce had a huge range but Blaze has a deep voice instead. We understand you have that impression with songs from Bruce's period that he has to sing. Those are not songs that are written for his voice but he does the best he can. Some of these songs are really difficult to sing and every singer has trouble with such songs. Bruce had a two-octave range but Blaze really gives all that he's got. Personally, I don't like those falsetto voices. I rather like when everything comes from the deep and Blaze is [really] good at that.'

Embracing the notion of a creative fresh start in writing the album, Steve Harris said in the same conversation with a European rock journalist, '[We didn't] hark back to any of the old days. That's the key. You don't write a "Run to the Hills" part two, you just write the best set of songs at that time that you can. It's no good trying to think back or trying to think we should be doing stuff people expect. We've always been very stubborn about that sort of thing. We've written what we like and people can take it or leave it ... Blaze came in and asked what direction we are going in and I said we just do what we do. He said he had some ideas he wasn't sure about, and I told him to just write them and, if they worked, they worked. Luckily they did. In the end it fitted unbelievably. It really worked. It felt so right it was brilliant.'

Bayley added in an interview with journalist Sumit Chandra that one agreement the band and its new singer made was important in not repeating the past. 'Nothing was written for the album before I joined the band. So one thing was [that] we waited to write the material until I had joined the band, and we took our time and wrote the best songs we could. Then, when we got to recording, we went for a vibe thing, where we were trying to make sure that each track had a mood and feel of its own, and we put in the time to ensure that this happened.'

Another new dynamic the band had to contend with heading into recording was brought about by the exit of long-time producer Martin Birch. Rather than seeking out a hotshot metal producer of the time, the band decided they'd been at it long enough to be their own boss in the studio this time out. This, Blaze explained, translated to *The X Factor* being 'the first album Steve Harris had produced with Nigel Green. We also had some technical difficulties along the way that cost us a couple of weeks.'

Birch seemed to feel relaxed about handing over the production reigns to Harris. 'It was nothing against Maiden,' he recalled to band biographer Mick Wall. 'None of us are getting any younger and it was just time for me to get off the treadmill ... [By that point] Steve had become much more involved in the production side ... and he'd worked by my side for years on so many previous Maiden albums, I knew they'd be in safe hands.'

Responding to a question about his state of readiness to step up to the production plate, Steve Harris told *Shock Waves* magazine, 'I suppose I kind of co-produced the earlier albums and arranged the songs. In a way, I'm very glad I worked with Martin Birch on the previous albums because I learned a lot from it. I also mixed the two live albums, *A Real Live One* and *A Real Dead One*, because Martin decided to leave. So I had to hire an engineer and, fortunately, I had some experience in the studio.'

With change swirling around them as they headed into pre-production, new singer Blaze Bayley recalled to Sumit Chandra that no one in the band went unaffected by it. 'I think it was what going on around all of us, I suppose. There were a lot of changes for everybody in their lives ... Everybody was going through a bit of soul searching at the time, as far as what was happening in music and what was going to happen to the band with a new singer, and how it was all going to work out.'

Steve Harris recalled to a European rock journalist that 'When Blaze asked me what sort of direction we were going to go in, I said there was no direction. We just sit down and write the songs.' Still, Harris couldn't help but acknowledge that, because of what 'Blaze'd been through [leaving former band Wolfsbane], and I'd just come through a divorce ... it was going to be dark in some ways.'

The state of the world outside of Iron Maiden held plenty of macabre muses for the band. As Bayley told Sumit Chandra, 'There were also a lot of things on the TV, like the war in the former Yugoslavia. It was a time when everybody felt that we were going to dig in and make this record happen. I think we all drew on the dark sides within ourselves and the dark side of the human spirit, and used that dark energy in a positive way. In that way, it's worked out really well.

'It's a record that takes a couple of listens really. You've got to give it time because it's a long record and it's a bit darker, which makes it a little bit more difficult to get into, rather than if there were a couple of lighter numbers to break things up. It's pretty intense and moody really, for the most part.'

Harris added a qualifier in that, while he felt the album was dark, 'I don't think it's depressing in a way. It's intense and I think that's a good thing because it's gonna make people react in some way or other so, in that sense, I think it's really good ... In some ways, it definitely reflects the darker side of the human spirit and, in some ways, metaphorically, the animal instincts that we've all got. I think maybe new and young fans can relate to that because you can fall in on yourself and become reflective, and you can sometimes live in those darker feelings, and I think people can relate to that.'

Delving into his first collaborative songwriting effort for the new LP, Bayley began by pointing out the obvious. 'My approach has been completely different to Bruce's. I must say that he was a fabulous singer – he brought a lot to Maiden both as composer and singer. I never dreamed of replacing him and I just tried to stay myself. I had to bring my own identity and temper, write my own music.

'Now I suggest ideas which may seem to go in a different direction but they are accepted because this band is opened to everything. And Steve is such a positive composer, who writes so many songs, especially on this album – his best up to now, I think – that it pushes you to transcend yourself and sing the best you can. Some of Steve's songs are so good that you hardly believe it. On this album you can feel that the music is played by guys who enjoy what they're doing without any compromise.

'Before I started working on the album I asked Steve if he wished to have a global direction. He told me, "No, no, let's go and see how it works. Let's start writing and the album will take shape." And what a shape! I co-wrote five tracks and wrote some others by myself. I'd say that I worked on eight or ten tracks.'

For Harris, that process of letting the album take shape began when they started writing the songs. 'It was very natural. We didn't really have any specific topics or anything. We never do. Whenever we do a new album, we really have no idea what we're going to write about. We have little bits of musical ideas that we stick on tape and then forget about until we pull them out when it's time to do an album.

'When we're on the road we don't get much of a chance to do anything, except to sleep on days off and things like that. We don't write on the road. So, therefore, it's quite exciting when we do a new album because we never know what we're going to do. That's part of the fun of it. We don't know what the topics or the songs are going to be. It's very fresh and exciting, especially working with a new guy, and it worked so well. It was so natural writing songs with him. It was almost as if he'd been in the band for ages.'

Bayley's openness to being a team member was a big plus in this respect. 'I like to collaborate with other people,' he told Sumit Chandra. 'Generally, I've got an idea for a lyric or melody that I want to get across. You bring this idea to everybody and see how it works out. Janick also does the same thing as far as bringing ideas to the group. When Steve gets an idea, he likes to get the whole thing finished and then bring it to rehearsal and work on the arrangements. That's great and it's really enjoyable to sing those songs because they have a really unique feel that only Steve can get, and it brings out a part of my voice that I would normally not get to.'

Bayley also recalled a completely out-of-the-box approach to writing the album. 'This first came up during a talk with Steve when I asked him when we'd start recording demos. He answered, "What demos? We never do any demos – we rehearse in the studio instead. All we do is play until we feel it's good and then we record." Many times it didn't work but it didn't matter. I felt like a real idiot but, when the recording was over, I had the feeling [of having] recorded a demo with all the qualities of a finished product. It was incredible and sometimes we would stop the song right there because we didn't know how to end it. This way we kept the freshness and the spontaneity, and we got something really magical. Each song took us three or four days but, in the end, we knew it had something unique. This way to work was new for me but I got used to it. It's part of making our ideas progress and we found a new identity for the band.'

Once the band had begun principal tracking Bayley felt Harris 'started drawing ... my identity as a singer ... out of me and I learned more about myself ... [and] found [that] identity ... on this album.' Stepping into the shoes of a giant like Bruce Dickinson was no easy feat but Bailey seemed fired up by the challenge of the expectation among die-hard Maiden fans and it was clear he was keen to win them over.

Speaking about the vocal qualities he'd felt made Bayley right to replace Bruce Dickinson's signature wail, Steve Harris recalled of the audition that 'he got the job on merit ... In my eyes, I felt he would be the right man.'

Though Bayley quickly earned his new bandmates' respect, he admitted later, 'I doubted myself at first because it seemed like such a momentous thing. And if you think about what Bruce did – fantastic voice, incredible range, the songs that he sung – and about what Paul [Di'Anno] did when he was in the band, trying to follow those two geezers ...

'I already had power and aggression but my personality is more visible now, with more intensity and emotion. I only came close to this before but, with Maiden, everything came naturally. I think that Steve has found this unexpected skill thanks to his songs because I had been unable to do so when I was writing alone ... So I was glad I jumped through all the hoops because I was then sure of myself and it made me feel better.'

Guitarist Dave Murray added, in an interview with Maidenfans.com, 'On *The X Factor* [Blaze's] voice was recorded a lot drier. Blaze didn't get a lot of favours. His voice sounded naked, like it is and that's OK for me because I think he sounds brilliant, with loads of deep sounds. In a lot of rock music the vocals are recorded with a lot of effects, by which they are absorbed in the entire. But on *The X Factor* it was good to do it differently. Maybe it wasn't right for his voice but, for that record, it had to be done this way.'

By the time the band had concluded recording Bayley recalled to Sumit Chandra, they had 'over eighty minutes of music for the album and, when you go through the mixing process, it adds additional time to the effort. Also we had a new sound now with the new singer ... Overall, it was the first album that we had done together as a band and we wanted to take the time to make it as right as it could be. So we kept on pushing to make it the best we could and we're all happy with the result.'

Bayley also revealed that the band had even recorded some

covers, including the Who's classic 'My Generation' and UFO's 'Doctor, Doctor'. 'We just strolled through Steve's record collection, as the studio is on the side of his house, and just looked to see what we knew, and then took some time in the studio and knocked them out. So it was a bit of fun really.'

Working with a new front man and a new producer weren't the only changes the band faced with *The X Factor*. They also had a new label, independent CMC International, which had been a haven of sorts for fellow metal major-label ex-pats like Judas Priest and Yngwie Malmsteen. Rather than viewing the departure from EMI as a step down, the band embraced the chance of a fresh start, as Bayley explained to Sumit Chandra.

'Maiden was out of a deal and CMC really wanted Maiden to go with them. I think they've stuck with what heavy rock is all about. They're not trying to get the bands to write commercial hits, or trying to get the bands to tone down or soften up in any way. And it's good to be with a label that's like that. They're very enthusiastic about the band and the new record so that's been a really good move. The main reason for bringing out the back catalogue with all the B-sides is so that everything is on the same standard of quality, and everything's been remastered for release on CD.'

With a new record label and a new singer in place, Steve Harris told a European rock journalist prior to the album's release, 'When Blaze joined, it was like we were a band again. Whenever we've had a changeover in the band, it's been very quick and none too painful. This was different and weird. It took me back to when it was just me and Dave and Doug Sampson, and we had no singer and we were rehearsing.'

Though feeling on a personal level as if he'd successfully set Maiden off on to their next voyage, Harris admitted, 'I always worry about how people are going to react to our albums. Probably more so with this one than any of the others because it's so important. But I always worry, always will do. The time that you get that big headed that you think, "Oh, we're gonna sell so many albums," – well, that's the time to give up, I suppose.

'You've always got to be worried. If someone writes some bullshit about you in the paper, slags your album off, which, to be honest, has never really happened to us – we've always been pretty lucky with the press but nobody likes to be slagged off. You can say you don't care but you really do. Obviously you want to be liked, and you spend a lot of time putting your heart and soul into an album, and you want it to be appreciated. But then again, you can't expect everyone out there to like Iron Maiden.'

With the released of *The X Factor* on 2 October 1995 *Rolling Stone* reported that Iron Maiden had successfully 'weathered its numerous personnel changes without a hitch'. MTV added that, while the record failed to chart as well as some of its predecessors, despite producing two singles in 'Man on the Edge' (which made No. 10 in the UK) and 'Lord of the Flies', it was still a success in England.

Years later, co-producer Nigel Green reflected to

Maidenfans.com on how the title wound up being so fitting as the band embarked on a new stage in their 20-year-old career. 'We all felt that the way things were progressing – the songs, Blaze's new involvement, the sound, the commitment – the new album really would have that extra quality, that bit of magic, that X factor. This became the working title for the album and we liked it so we kept it. It is also very apt as this is our tenth studio album.'

In talking about the success of the band's first album since the departure of Bruce Dickinson, Steve Harris seemed at peace with the result. In an interview with *Kerrang!* he said that the album, at its core, reflected, as with any new Iron Maiden album, that 'what we do is from the heart. *The X Factor* did a million worldwide. That's great, I'll have that.'

Still, Harris acknowledged that, when the new line-up first hit the road, the unknowns the band were facing for the first time were still fresh in the pit of his stomach. As he recalled to *Metal Hammer*, 'We had a new singer and the vibe we were getting from the outside world was that Iron Maiden were dead but we did it against the odds. We were desperate to prove people wrong.

'I'll be honest, there were some places like America where we thought, "Fucking hell, have we still got an audience?" because we hadn't played there for four years. And they were still loyal so this time we're gonna go back and do the sheds [arenas]. People out there would even ask us, "Are you still valid?" And we'd reply, "Yeah, we're still valid to ourselves and our fans, and that's all we care about."'

For Harris, at the end of the day, it was about the fans over any other consideration. 'We freely admit that we've made enough money to be comfortable but we keep doing this because we want to do it.'

CHAPTER ELEVEN

VIRTUAL XI (1998)

'Bad reviews are only irritating when they're not constructive'
Steve Harris

'With the past three or four albums, we've left off anything that we weren't a hundred per cent certain about.
Steve Harris

Having weathered most of the mid-1990s – metal's dark time – as an indie band, by 1998 Iron Maiden seemed confident that they were on the right track by sticking to their musical guns, rather than trying to conform to popular musical trends.

As a band who had always been the one setting and maintaining those trends, within the context of the heavy-metal genre they'd helped pioneer over the two decades prior, Iron Maiden were doing just that once again, only this time by *proving* that metal still had a loyal following when few other bands of their generation were able. While Metallica had the luxury of having gone pop, bands like Slayer and Iron Maiden stuck to their stylistic guns, and it was a gamble the band was beginning to see pay off as they rolled out their second LP with new lead singer Blaze Bayley.

As he told *Format Power* magazine, 'When we released our last album, everyone said that grunge had killed metal. Bands like Alice in Chains and Soundgarden – all of those guys said that metal was dead but instead all those bands have died out ... People are getting interested in metal bands again. Iron Maiden have always had the same kind of roots and identity to the sound but were always trying to experiment with writing, creating new ideas and different formats for songs. I believe that metal is back.'

Guitarist Dave Murray added to *Terrorizer* magazine, 'To me, it's almost come full circle again. That mid-1980s vibe is happening, it's actually coming back. Because sometimes people need to grab something solid musically and I think there was a period in the last few years where there's been a real gaping hole.'

Regardless of their popularity, Steve Harris felt that, by that point in the band's career, they had a signature sound and he saw no reason to tinker with it, stating candidly to *Metal Hammer*, 'We weren't trying to be current, or retro or anything. People will either love this kind of music or hate it but we just take each song in any direction that feels natural.'

Heading into the songwriting for the band's 11th studio album guitarist Dave Murray told Maidenfans.com that, as always, the process began with Harris. 'He has his own way of songwriting and playing bass. He's the centre of everything. He has very clear ideas when he writes a song.' Harris himself told journalist Sumit Chandra that, by that point in more than 20 years as a songwriter, 'It's like a good wine in that you definitely get better with age. I definitely feel

Above: A 1980 publicity opportunity for Iron Maiden at Madame Tussauds wax museum.

Below: Maiden in 1980: Clive Burr, Dave Murray, Steve Harris, Dennis Stratton
nd Paul Di'Anno.

Above: Backstage in 1983 with Adrian Smith, Steve Harris, Bruce Dickinson. © *Getty Imag*

Below: Maiden in full live effect. © *Rex Featur*

Dave Murray's guitar amp and rig. © *Tony Mottram*

Above: Bruce Dickinson.
© Tony Mottram

Right: Blaze Bayley replaced Dickinson as lead vocalist in the 1990s. *© Rex Features*

bove left: Dave Murphy in the studio. *© Rex Features*

bove right: Nicko McBrain in the studio Steve Harris built in his Essex
ırm Barnyard. *© Tony Mottram*

elow left: Steve Harris. *© Tony Mottram*

elow right: Dave Murray in Harris's studio. *© Getty Images*

Above left: Preparing Eddie for the live show. © *Tony Mottram*

Above right: The launch party for *Seventh Son of a Seventh Son* in Germany. © *Tony Mottram*

Below: The mixing desk shooting *Raising Hell* at Pinewood. © *Tony Mottram*

Above: Maiden producer Martin Birch, here flanked by Ronnie Dio and Ritchie Blackmore of Rainbow. *© Getty Images*

Below: Acts produced by Kevin Shirley included Led Zeppelin, Journey, Dream Theater and, right, Tyler Bryant. *© Getty Images*

Above: Live in Scotland in 2006 – Adrian Smith, Dave Murray and Janick Gers.

© Rex Feature

Below: The band in 2009.

© Rex Feature

like that. You can't say it's like a sports figure where the body deteriorates but in music it's much different – you can definitely mature and get better.

'Some people will talk about liking a certain part of our history. We've got a very long past. So even if somebody got into the band three albums ago, they tend to talk about that era. Most fans talk with great fondness about the first album they got into of any band. The situation you have now is that you may have new young fans that have recently gotten into the band, and you ask them about their favourite album and they usually mention the first one they heard. They go out and buy all the others as well but it's usually the album that they got into first that remains special. So, if you ask someone that got into the band since the first or second album, that is the period they feel the most fondness for.

'You can't compete with that, not just because of the music but also because of the time period they got into. They may have fond memories of the girlfriend they were with or other events that happened which are associated with that time period and you can never compete with that, regardless of what you do with a new album. You can't worry about that ... [you] just do the best job you possibly can.'

When the subject turned to collaboration in the band's songwriting, Harris told *Metal Hammer*, 'Despite what some ex-members of the band would have you believe, I am open minded. Fans have always been secondary – I don't mean that in a bad way – but, if you don't put your own enjoyment and satisfaction first, you'll end up rewriting 'The Number of the Beast' ten times over because that's their favourite song.

I'm up for doing most things song-wise ... but they have to be good ideas.'

Offering further testimony of Harris's open-mindedness in the writing process, Blaze Bayley remarked to Metal-Rules.com, 'One of the first things that I said to Steve Harris when I joined the band was, "Is anyone else going to be involved in this and are we going to be forced to write hit singles or something like that?" And he said, "No. It is just us in the band. No one says anything about this music apart from us. That is it! No one has any say or control over this." And I thought, "Right. That suits me." It's just perfect.'

When it came to collaborations with other band members on the new album, Bayley said, 'I worked again with Janick and also had a chance to work with Dave Murray. Dave came up to my house. We were talking about this idea on the last US tour and I said, "Dave, I've got this idea and we must work on it." Then, when it came time for writing, we got together and it did pan out. We had a couple of ideas which turned out really good but that was the best one, and we decided to record that and put it on the record.'

Guitarist Murray told Maidenfans.com of the band's songwriting, 'Most of the times it happens spontaneously when we're writing. The chemistry in the band changed when Blaze joined. It's also a matter of vibrations. You can work with some people and with others you can't. In a band it's just the same and, if we hit it off, we write things in a special way and it gives the right sparks.'

Musically, Blaze added to *Format Power* that, as the band wrote, they all kept in mind that 'melody is very important, whether it's in the guitar or the vocals. Words must be interesting and to come up with a good melody is essential with a good verse. We don't just stick guitars in – it's mix and match. When we write songs, we do consider the live performances – we even see imagery when we are writing.'

For Harris, his lifelong love of football provided one lyrical muse. As he told *Shockwave* magazine, 'Over the last couple years in particular, more and more young kids are getting into soccer, not so much here [the US] but in the rest of the world people are soccer mad! Especially in places like Italy, Spain and South America. We headlined the Monsters of Rock festival on our last tour and, when we played Sao Paulo (Brazil), I would wear Brazil's soccer shirt and, when we were in Argentina, we would wear the Argentina jersey. The fans over there give us loads of shirts because they know how much we're into soccer and the fans get so into it.

'So we thought it would be great if we could tie the two together ... It's our eleventh album, the World Cup is coming up and we're totally into soccer. So to tie in with *Virtual XI* we have the five members of the band and the eleven is made up of six international soccer players. It's great fun and it's brilliant for me because of my love for soccer.'

Dave Murray put such talk into perspective when he told Maidenfans.com about the new album's subject matter. 'Some songs are about computers, technology, science and virtual reality. This is the end of the twentieth century and of a millennium. The soccer theme is present – we all love football – but it certainly isn't the main theme. But there are similarities between a rock and a football audience. They're all the same kinds of people: singing and wearing flags. In some parts of our songs there are themes that can be heard in a football stadium.'

Delving into the inspiration behind some of the album's tracks, Blaze Bayley told journalist Sumit Chandra that 'Two Worlds Collide' was 'about the extinction of the human race due to an object coming from outer space and, by sheer coincidence, there are two movies, *Armageddon* and *Deep Impact*, that talk about the same thing.

'"Two Worlds" also is about cultures clashing. In our travels we get to see many cultures and see how different cultures clash. An example of that is our last visit to Argentina, where I saw the memorial to the soldiers that died in the Falklands War. It's a Latin culture, the people are really friendly, it was very sobering.'

Steve Harris added to IronMaidenCommentary.com of the song's genesis, 'This was from an idea by Dave, who worked with Blaze, and then I worked with both of them, adding parts to the music, part of the chorus melody line and arranging the song. Dave wrote most of the music and Blaze wrote the lyrics.'

Murray added, in an interview with Maidenfans.com, 'In the solar system there are a lot of things flying like asteroids and meteors and those things could hit each other or our Earth. It's about collisions that can lead to the destruction of one form of life and maybe start a new one.'

Of 'The Educated Fool', Murray offered to Maidenfans.com that the song, at its core, was 'about us – people. Actually, we all are a bit educated fools. It's about self-analysis and going deeper into the meaning of things. This song has got all those tempo changes that only Maiden can do. Other bands try that too but they can't do it like Maiden can.'

Harris added to Ironmaidencommentary.com, '"The Educated Fool" started from the guitar melody line that you hear at the beginning and it fitted really well with a couple of other ideas that I had at the time. It turned out very strong and is one of Blaze's favourites on the album.'

For the layout of 'The Clansman', Murray explained to *Terrorizer* magazine, 'I made a few suggestions, and we all contributed slightly to the arrangements and everything. I think it's going to be a great song, you know. The imagery on "The Clansman" – when you listen to it, it makes you feel ... It's a "wind in your hair" sort of vibe and I think Steve's captured that within the song. It'll actually take you to that place. Say you're reading a book – the imagery that you can get from reading – in this instance the music really works and it takes you there.'

Harris added to Ironmaidencommentary.com that 'The Clansman' had started as 'two separate ideas, then we put them together and it worked! It's got a Celtic flavour to the music, which is why I wrote the lyrics about the Scottish clans. They [the lyrics] were inspired also by the *Braveheart* and *Rob Roy* films.'

Drawing on a real-life historical inspiration for 'Como Estás Amigos,' Dave Murray told Maidenfans.com that the song harked back to 'people we met during the Falklands War Memorial. It's about how politicians divide those people in camps. If you personally meet the inhabitants of countries at war, they're people just like you and me.'

Steve Harris added to IronMaidencommentary.com, 'This was written by Jan and Blaze, with Jan writing the music and Blaze the vocal melody lines and lyrics. It's a sad but powerful song, quite dark but dramatic, about the Falklands War. I think it makes an excellent album closer.'

Of 'The Angel and the Gambler', the bassist/songwriter recalled to *Shockwave* that spontaneous inspiration had popped into his head. 'When I came up with that song idea, I put it on a mini tape recorder while I was driving down the motorway and I distinctly remember saying to myself, "This reminds me of the Who meets UFO." So I just took it in that direction.' He added to IronMaidenCommentary.com that, musically, 'It's got a very 1970s rhythm feel to it, which I like a lot.'

Singling out 'Futreal' as an example of 'an idea that I'd had for quite some time but hadn't worked up into a full song until the writing started for this album', Harris added in the same conversation that, from there, 'I worked up all the music and vocal melody lines but I didn't have a suitable lyric so I asked Blaze to write something for it, and very fine it is too!'

'Don't Look to the Eyes of a Stranger', he continued, was 'another idea which I'd had for a while but hadn't managed to work up into a full song until now. I wanted it to sound a bit orchestral as it had a majestic feel to it. It also sounded very ominous so I wanted to make the end part completely mad and manic. I think Jan's not too sure about that part but I think it works great!'

Dave Murray offered to Maidenfans.com that 'Heaven Can Wait' 'symbolises, for me, the 1990s in that young people don't play football any more but they watch it or play a computer game. That's an important form of alienation in our society – at least that's our impression of the time we live in.'

Finally, Steve Harris credited 'Lightning Strikes Twice' as originating, musically, with Murray. 'This started as an initial idea of Davey's, and we just picked it up from there and worked it into a complete song together. I wrote the lyrics after coming up with the words for the chorus during the arranging of the music with Dave. He liked the idea of the title so I wrote the lyrics around that.'

As the band finished pre-production Murray recalled to Maidenfans.com, 'Everyone had his contributions with little pieces and, once we had brought order into everything, it went quickly to record. The actual recordings took us only three weeks and the rest was "finishing" – using loads of technologies ... The new album is obviously different and that's the way it has to be – each record has to be different. We used a lot of technologies on this one but, wisely, it's not a computer record.'

Indeed, Blaze Bayley revealed to *Terrorizer*, 'This album is a lot more spontaneous from the recording point of view because we had much less rehearsal and we attempted to get the songs on to tape a lot earlier than we did on *The X Factor*.'

When the band entered the recording phase, they tracked once again from the comforts of Steve Harris' Barnyard Studios. As Blaze Bayley told Metal-Rules.com, 'The advantage of doing it that way is that there is nobody else around really. It's just about you and your band. Everybody that's there is working on the same project and that is good. It makes for a much more relaxed atmosphere but it is much more than that. It is focused because you are only there to do that one thing.

'We used a lot of new technology on this album as well. We recorded direct to hard drive using Virtual Tracks and a new system from Soundscape. Every time we had a bug in it they e-mailed us the solution and we downloaded it right from the Internet. It was great really ... We use absolutely the cutting edge at the moment. I mean, we use the same instruments but, to get the representation of the music that we want, we use only the latest stuff. There is definitely a theme of technology that surrounds the album but Iron Maiden would seem to have a very human heart remaining.

'The way we look at writing songs is that technology is a tool and that is all that it is. It is not creative on its own. It comes from inside you really. Sometimes you can be inspired because you are playing a different guitar or you have found an interesting sound on an instrument or something but the way that we write songs is by getting together and working things out – chords and vocals, and trying to get some interesting lyrics together. That is the human side of it – that and real drums and guitars and vocals. I think that is it really. Technology is a tool but it can just turn you around in circles if you start to rely on it.'

As the band rolled tape in a landscape that was rapidly moving from analogue to digital recording Blaze told

Terrorizer magazine, 'It's an evolution as well, for Steve as a producer. I think the sound is a lot more guitar-orientated, in the way that the guitars are forward a lot more, but the bass is still there. But I think, maybe from a production point of view, Steve has pieced this together and made the sound reflective of a different kind of vibe.'

Talking about where keyboards had helped to round out certain tracks on the album, Harris told *Metal Hammer*, 'There are no more keyboards than usual, they're just further up in the mix. On "The Clansman" and "Don't Look to the Eyes of a Stranger" we wanted a very orchestral sound and I actually played the keyboards myself – it was quicker that way. We've used keyboards in the past but this time we really took it to the max and it came out well. Nicko always moans about using keyboards because he wants to keep it rock 'n' roll but he rang to say how great the Hammond organ sounded on "The Angel and the Gambler".'

In the same interview Dave Murray detailed how the band had worked through the construction of the album's complicated parts. 'We kept a lot of the original bass and guitar tracks, and some of the vocals that we actually put down originally. We didn't wipe the slate clean after the drums were put down. We did some rebuilding and Steve kept a lot of his bass, and it was just a case of patching up things and then laying on the guitar melodies and the harmonies, and then the vocals. But there's a lot of colour, if you like, in the sound there. It's got a depth to it, where you can play it over and over, and hear something new each time.'

When attention turned to tracking the album's vocals, Blaze Bayley shared his feeling with *Shockwave* that he'd grown as a vocalist since *The X Factor*. 'I learned so much about the different areas of my voice and I made it stronger.' From a technical point of view, Murray recalled that Bayley's voice was 'recorded with a lot [of] additional equipment', which the band took advantage of on tracks like 'The Clansman'. The singer told *Terrorizer*, 'It was good doing it in the studio because there was a lot of banter around that track. When we were coming up with it and making suggestions and different things, it was a real group effort.'

Released on 23 March 1998, *Virtual XI* marked the band's lowest sales and charting points in years, even though *Billboard* concluded that Iron Maiden had still delivered 'all the crunching riffs and demonic horror of their best records'. The band felt they had grown by musical leaps and bounds since their last studio LP, with guitarist Dave Murray telling *Terrorizer*, 'I think *Virtual XI* is superior to *The X Factor* ... [which] was Steve's first go as a producer and Blaze had just joined the band as well. So it was all new.'

Elaborating on the differences a world tour had made in getting the band's players fully familiar with one another, Blaze Bayley told *Terrorizer*, 'This is a much more confident album. At the start of *The X Factor* this line-up of the band hadn't toured together and there were a whole lot of expectations surrounding it. Now, with the start of *Virtual XI*, we've done a world tour together, we have a very successful album behind us and we released *Best of the Beast* as well. Everybody's looking forward to the future and feeling confident, and I think that's a big part of the sound.'

As for Steve Harris, he acknowledged to *Kerrang!* that he'd been 'really wound up' by the album's indifferent reception – 'I'd just spent a year of my life working silly hours doing this album – which I still love and I don't give a fuck what anyone says.' Looking toward the Millennium, however, he told *Metal Hammer* that things looked bright for the band because 'the spirit of musical freedom is very healthy. And, hopefully, we'll fit in with all that too. All we need is for people to be a bit more open minded. If there's this vibe of anything goes, surely that gives us as good a chance as anybody.'

The work the band had invested in maintaining its fan base over the past decade was clearly reflected in Harris's humbled outlook on the band's future. The millennium would pay Iron Maiden back handsomely for the work they'd put into keeping their fans entertained via new studio LPs, video games featuring their music, the online fan presence they'd built via their official interactive website, as well as fansites around the world. Having laid the groundwork for what would follow with all of the aforementioned, the Beast was about to rise again as the band headed into a *brave new world* ...

CHAPTER TWELVE

BRAVE NEW WORLD (2000)

'(*Brave New World*) is a step forward for classic heavy metal' CMJ

'It was like we'd never been apart! It felt like the band had never split in loads of directions. It was very natural – very comfortable – and there was a spark there, and a glimmer in everyone's eyes' Dave Murray

'The record does have a kind of progressive element to it, which is very rare in this day and age' Bruce Dickinson

'Producers Kevin Shirley and Steve Harris give the recordings a white-hot intensity' iTunes.com

Throughout the 1990s every sub-genre of rock, from hair metal and grunge to alternative rock and rap rock, had experienced a roller-coaster ride of commercial peak followed by plummeting decline. Metal, meanwhile, had sustained itself commercially through a coupling of fan loyalty and bands – from Megadeth and Slayer to Testament – making records that didn't stray far from their genre's core sound.

Iron Maiden had arguably been a leader in this trend and

had succeeded, despite what many viewed as the handicap of Dickinson's absence. Maiden's fans had stuck by them in spite of all the odds and, as a result, Iron Maiden had successfully survived much of the decade without their long-time lead singer Bruce Dickinson.

Though the band had released three mid-1990s albums with Blaze Bayley handling lead vocals, and while each of those releases had gone platinum, it was clear that fans' patience was running a bit short as they desired the full experience of vintage Maiden as the band for their buck. Though bands like Journey and Van Halen had succeeded with replacements – in Journey's case, a Japanese tribute singer-soundalike for front man Steve Perry and, in Halen's case, a poppier reinvention with classic rock staple Sammy Hagar. Being part of a less commercial genre, Iron Maiden was also experiencing a new generation of fans discovering their classic material for the first time, through the band's interactive video game *Flight 666* and the phenomenon of downloading music. Regardless of the gateway, it was clear that millions of old and new metal fans alike around the globe wanted their classic Maiden line-up back.

To satisfy demand the band reunited in 1999, entering the studio to create an album that Popmatters.com would say embodied an 'energy that matches older records like *Piece of Mind* or *The Number of the Beast*'.

According to guitarist Dave Murray in a conversation with *Rolling Stone* in early 1999, that family reunion began when 'we approached Bruce and Adrian a few months ago to feel it out and see if they would be interested because their solo things are going quite nicely. It was immediate from them – the response was a hundred percent "Yes!"'

Elaborating, Dickinson explained in an interview with Triple JJJ FM Radio in March 1999 that 'we share, Maiden and myself, the same manager Rod Smallwood and he obviously knows what's going on in my head and what's going on in the Maiden guys' [heads] as well. We had a chat one day and he said, "Look, Blaze is leaving the band. How do you feel about ... if you wanted to come back?" And I was like, "Well, you go talk to Steve. I'd be up for it but we should all get together and have a chat."

'So we all got together for a meeting down at Brighton, which is where Rod lives, and had an afternoon down there, and afternoon turned into an evening down the pub and, by that time, it was all over. It didn't take long, you know, to wander in and say ... There wasn't a huge amount to discuss apart from, "Let's get on with it." ... Steve was concerned that I didn't want to do it for five minutes, and grab the money and run, and I said, "No, that's not the intention." My concern was [that] we really have to make a great record.'

Expanding on his initial concerns, Steve Harris told journalist Don Kaye that, first and foremost, 'We want this to be a long-term thing. The first thing I said to Bruce was, "Why do you want to come back?" and the second thing was, "How long are you staying for?" We didn't want him coming back to do a one-off tour and that's it. We'd rather get someone else. And that's what we probably would have done if Bruce's attitude hadn't been right and we didn't believe that he was coming back for the long term.'

The singer, for his part, told *Metal Hammer* magazine that his decision to rejoin Iron Maiden was an emotional one for everyone in the band. 'When we got back in the room together, me and Steve gave each other a great big hug. He's only ever hugged me three times in my life! Fantastic and great fun. We were all looking forward to making great music and having a phenomenally good time. It was great.'

To round out the band's powerhouse line-up, Harris added, 'After that it was more or less my idea to get Adrian back. If Bruce was definitely coming back, it felt right to have Adrian back as well.'

Expanding on the decision to take on a third guitarist, Dave Murray recalled in an interview with an Iron Maiden fansite, 'As soon as Bruce came down and started singing with the band, and Adrian as well started playing, it was obvious, musically, it was going to work. Actually, we made the decision before we played together.'

The band's third guitarist, Janick Gers, told Ironmaiden.com of Smith rejoining the fold, 'I have [kept in touch] with Adrian and it's going to be really interesting with three guitars. I don't know how they're going to fit us all on stage but it's going to be a very powerful sound and we're all really excited about it.'

Gers also gave his candid opinion to *Rock On* that it was simply no contest between Blaze and Bruce in terms of singing abilities. 'Iron Maiden have their identity but Bruce was their face and it was hard to substitute. Blaze came. There's no comparison between Bruce's and Blaze's voice! Even he [Bayley] admits this. That which is important is that he loved the band and gave his best for it. Bruce has an incredible range of almost three octaves. There was no chance, therefore, that Blaze could have reached Bruce's standards and that had bigger cost for the live shows ... Bruce's technique is definitely greater because, try as he might have, Blaze didn't have the technical foundations Bruce has.'

Talking about the three-guitar sound that everyone immediately compared to Lynyrd Skynyrd, Steve Harris told Ironmaiden.com, 'I think it's going to be really exciting to have Bruce and Adrian back. I'm very excited that there are six people in the band. Three guitar players and all that – I'm looking forward to it a lot. As far as I know, there's no one in metal or rock that's really done the three guitar thing, apart from Skynyrd. I really like the Skynyrd stuff – not that it'll be like that but it should be interesting.'

Bruce Dickinson, in the same conversation, added his feeling that 'The characters of the three guitarists actually blend very well. Jan has this completely anarchic style, which, in a sense, can now be set free, as before he had to fulfil Adrian's parts and his parts. Davey has a very distinct style. They all have. They're all capable of being as disciplined as they need to be but they've all got such separate personalities that it's going to be fantastic. I think, with Adrian back in the band, he's going to make such a huge contribution. Having worked with him, he's as good, if not better, than he ever was.

'There's always work for three guitars in a Maiden song, simply because of the number of guitars that we laid down in the studio that we never ever do live. In actual fact, the old Maiden songs will sound even better with three guitars.'

Dave Murray added his opinion in the same conversation. 'I suppose Skynyrd are one of the only bands around with that sort of line-up. With Maiden, on the material side of it, it really weighs [in] favour between guitars. In fact, there's a lot of stuff on the studio albums with three guitar harmonies anyway and that's most of the old material so we'll be able to incorporate that ... It's going to widen and give it another dimension. Sometimes they say less is more but I think, in this case, more is heavier! More is going to be bigger so I'm really looking forward to it and the thing is, with Adrian, it's going to widen the whole scope musically, where we can do more things within the band musically, so I think it's going to take shape very well.

'Subconsciously, I think we will write differently also. It'll be there in the back of your head because you can actually add things in there. I think it's going to affect things – slightly – it'll make things a lot broader, in some sense, but that we're yet to find out. I really think it's going to work great. It'll broaden the sound and make it damn fat!

'I think the chemistry within the band has increased with getting Bruce and Adrian back. The magic that was there before, I think we can recreate again. There was something still there from X amount of years ago between us and, getting back together, there's a real excitement. It's a kind of excitement between everybody. You can really feel it and I think it's going to be great. There's so much chemistry with this line-up now.'

For his part, Adrian Smith offered in the same group interview that playing with the band again felt great. 'It's great to be playing back with the guys again. Everyone's relaxed and happy about it, and we're looking forward to playing all the classic Maiden songs on this tour. It's kind of uncanny. I've seen everyone individually over the years but it's the first time we've all been together in a working situation for a long time. It must be almost eight years. We built up our own language over a period of time. We fell back into that straight away.'

In terms of writing songs, Bruce Dickinson put concerns over rekindling the creative chemistry to rest in an interview with rock journalist Vinnie Apicella. 'We went right back to how we wrote the songs fifteen years ago. We all went and lived in the same place for three months [with] everybody knocking on each others doors and writing individual bits. Then we all got together in one room and presented songs, and that's pretty much how the record got made ... with everybody writing with everybody else. In fact, because there are six guys in the band now, and five of us are all writers, it means there's an awful lot of variety on the record.'

In fact, in a separate conversation with journalist Clay Marshall Dickinson joked, 'The trouble is, we've got five songwriters in the band,' adding that democracy was the only system that prevailed. 'I'd be more than happy to write all ten songs,' he quipped, 'but I think Steve might have something to say about that! There are about five other songwriting ideas at least between me and

Davey, and me and Adrian, and me and Janick, that are all terrific ideas.'

Of the band's individual songwriting relationships, Adrian Smith offered the insight that 'Janick and Bruce have also got a good working relationship. They are actually living in the same house so they're coming up with a lot of stuff. It just depends on how we are going to do it, whether we are all going to sit in a room. I think it would be fun to try that. We've never really done that, [having] everyone contribute something to a song ... I think that would be fantastic.

'Having said that, we want to make the best album so we'll pick the best songs. Band politics can be a sticky area. I think everyone is at the stage now where they want to express themselves. It's about expression.'

In the same conversation with journalist Johnny B, Steve Harris added that 'everyone is gonna have a different opinion' about which were the strongest songs. 'You've come out and said certain things about what you are hearing and feeling about this album but, when I talk to the next person, they might have a completely different opinion. They might say, "That one sounds the same as this one," or, "This one sounds like the one a few albums ago." Songs are the life blood of any band. That really is half the battle – well, most of the battle really. Having good songs is what will see you through. Songs and lyrics are sometimes about moods and how you are feeling at the time.'

As the band worked to refine the track listing for their most commercially and artistically important album in over a decade Bruce Dickinson told *Promethean Crusade* fanzine that in spring 1999 the band took 'three months to come up with the basic nuts and bolts. Then off to do the tour, and another six weeks rehearsing and refining them.'

Writing the album's lyrics was a duty that fell primarily to Dickinson and Steve Harris. As the latter explained to journalist Johnny B, 'It's pretty well split really,' although all band members keep their fans first and foremost in mind. 'Nine times out of ten, as we write, we may think that a certain song is a great album track but it wouldn't necessarily work live, then usually that is the case.'

Asked about his own lyrical inspirations for the band's newest material, Harris gave a familiar answer. 'You just write at the time whatever you're feeling at the time. You draw your influences from anything at the time – it could be films, books, history or circumstantial events, whatever. Or whatever you come up with out of your imagination at the time – that's what it is.

'You know, people kind of read into them all sorts of things. Sometimes they get it right, sometimes they don't. I think that's good that they have a bit of imagination. They are thinking what they perceive about the lyrics. It is great because the lyrics are obviously strong enough that they make them think.'

For Bruce Dickinson, this process – as he told *Promethean Crusade* – begins with 'the things that pop in your head when you hear the music or when you hear the riffs. Like with "Ghost of the Navigator", when Janick was playing the riff in its raw state, somewhere along the line I sort of went, "Vikings!" and said, "OK, Vikings – Vikings equals ships equals boats equals sailing equals navigating equals going ... navigating! I know about navigating a bit – OK, one thing about navigation: dead reckoning. You don't know where you're going but you do know where you've been. That's an interesting concept. What happens is that I wander around humming an awful lot. Getting a tune together is the easy bit sometimes; it's getting the philosophy of the song down and what it's about right.'

Expanding on his process, the singer added that, when writing, 'It's important to allow yourself some space to allow what you do to become part of you and that way either the other guys will work with it or go against it. What I've found with the stuff I've written so far is that it has nice clarity to it and that's very important to me because [with] this Maiden album [it] has got to be very clear what it's all about ... I'm just really in tune to the moment, trying to write good solid metal tunes that are gonna sound great with a good vibe. Then introduce them to the guys, and we'll all jam around a bit and see what they sound like in the flesh.'

Elaborating further in an interview with the Disseminated Group website, Dickinson said, 'Ultimately ... the world exists in your own mind or your soul or somewhere like that. And the way I see the world is totally unique to the way somebody else sees the world. I have no idea how they see the world unless they present it to me in the form of art or pictures or music or words for a kind of a look between one mind or soul and another. Because of that, the moment of creation, the moment you create a song it's like the moment a little light bulb goes on. You've got the essence of something or the spark of something. You really see a picture of the whole thing. That moment is priceless.

'The thing is, it's priceless but it's also exhausting in some way. It's a bit like shelling a very, very, very annoying nut. You spend fucking ages picking away at this little thing and then, suddenly, right at the middle is this horrible little nut. Holding it, you think, "I did all that work just for that?" But at the same time you think, "Wow! It's great finding it in the end." So, at the same time, it's satisfying and frustrating. It's like me. You work very hard but basically have the desire to be very lazy. Yeah, people say, "Oh, you must be a workaholic?" Yeah but I want to be lazy. I really, really, really want to be lazy. But some days I can't be lazy.

'There's really no way around it when you begin creativity, if you want to create something that's really cool. In life a lot of your decisions are made for you and there are other people to sweep you along. You can be swept up by the audience and everything but your creativity, it's your own creation. Or maybe you borrowed it from somebody else for a while. Can I put it this way? Creativity is everywhere. It's just your job to observe it and use it. And that – the ability to observe – is very rewarding.'

Once the basic songs had been fleshed out guitarist Janick Gers recalled to Metal-Rules.com in August 1999 that the band next got 'together on a couple of days and went through every song and said, "How can we improve this song, as opposed to just sticking another guitar on it?" I think that the maturity of each of us and the musical ability of each of us means that we don't have to get everything all equal and become all excited about who is going to get the solos and stuff. We can use the best bit of what we have in the songs and the songs sound better.

'Offstage I can't tell you because I am not out there but on stage I can hear everything. I can hear all three different guitars and all the different stuff. I can hear the three-part harmonies and all the underneath stuff, and that is exactly what we wanted to do. The only other band that really does that is Lynyrd Skynyrd but that is more of a country-rock band. I have never heard a band this heavy do it. I think that we have enough themes and threads going through the tunes where we can have that guitar, and really feel that we have made the band heavier and more colourful.'

As the focus turned to perfecting the album's elaborate guitar parts guitarist Adrian Smith admitted to Ironmaiden.com that 'arranging is the hard part' before adding that their work was made easier by the fact that, 'If ever there was a band where three guitars could complement the music, it is Maiden. There are a lot of guitar harmonies and guitar parts. The songs are long and I think there's a lot of space there for three guitar players. It will complement the music, and it's never really been done before in the rock and metal field – obviously Skynyrd but I don't think in the metal field it's been done, which gives it an exciting dimension. I think it will sound amazing as we all play slightly differently ... I don't think it means we're going to have ninety-eight guitar solos in each song – I think it'll be more of a textural thing.'

Fellow guitarist Janick Gers added that the process of

blending all three players' parts and styles into one was 'really interesting because of the aesthetics of it. You can actually double up in various chords and stuff so we can make it a kind of bigger sound in various parts. The galloping parts will be the same but probably distinctly heavier because of the extra part there. There may be various parts where we might leave the bass and the two guitars might go off and might have a rhythm under them. And obviously where we can add three-part harmonies – that would be real fun to do. There are quite a lot of different things we can actually put into the songs and bring them into the year 2000!'

Steve Harris expanded on that process to an Iron Maiden fansite. '[With] some of the solos you would double them up and put one just in front of the other. It's a good effect! There is some of our earlier material where we did have three guitars on the album. We can actually do that now. It sounds really full, really good.'

Dave Murray added in the same conversation that, with three guitarists, 'We can incorporate the three guitar part harmonies, which is really good because sometimes we have left the three-part off an album just because we couldn't equate it live. This time we are actually doubling up on some of the solos, which is very good so it's made it more interesting. It's made it damn heavier.'

Drummer Nicko McBrain added that the sonic result was 'Chaos! Absolute chaos! First of all, I think it ... [brings] an added strength that has previously been untapped. We know that Adrian's guitar style worked for so many years with the band and then, when Janick came in, his style of playing is quite fiery and very effervescent compared to Adrian, who's more laid back and a more controlled player. We've got the best of both worlds there.'

In answer to the question of what Maiden sounded like with three guitars, Janick Gers told Iron Maiden.com, 'From my point of view, it sounds like classic Iron Maiden but much heavier! We have been working on some very interesting three-part harmonies, which really adds more texture to the songs in a live situation. There are also some great dual solos on some songs. It's definitely not like we've just added another guitar to sound louder – there is a real difference without losing that essential Maiden feel. As everyone knows, Adrian is a very creative guitarist and, on certain songs, he down-tunes his guitar, which adds to the bottom end of the sound, which makes it very heavy, adding a real depth and texture and modern sound without being grungy. The whole picture now seems very complete.'

Before discussing individual songs on the band's comeback LP, Bruce Dickinson began with the overall situation, telling journalist Clay Marshall, 'There's no theme to the album as a whole. It's a collection of songs. Steve's songs are pretty much on the dark side. Certainly some of the songs he's co-written with other people tend to be fairly lengthy, like eight to nine minutes, and almost quite prog-rocky in places as well. There's lots of atmospherics – "Rime of the Ancient Mariner"-style stuff but, actually, in my opinion, much better than "Rime of the Ancient Mariner". He's really developed his whole thing on this record and he has written some fucking great lyrics.

'There's a song called "Dream of Mirrors" and there's a lyric in that chorus – huge chorus – and the lyric is, "I only dream in black and white / I only dream because I'm alive / I only dream in black and white / to save me from myself", which is like, "Whoa!" He's getting pretty deep on some of this stuff.

'There's "The Mercenary" – it's about mercenaries. Generally, mercenaries are a bad thing. What can you say? There are all levels going on here. But "Dream of Mirrors" is fantastic and "Blood Brothers" I just think is a fucking masterpiece. It's the only song he's written on his own on this record.'

'Blood Brothers' has all the signatures of a classic Steve Harris/Iron Maiden classic and Dickinson described it as 'a little masterpiece' to *Classic Rock* magazine. 'In singing it I can tell you what I think it's about. It's about Steve's relationship with his father, who died. It's a very personal song so this song is about Steve and his father being blood brothers, like, for ever. The lines go: "Just for a second a glimpse of my father I see / and in a movement he beckons to me / and in a moment the memories are all that remain / and all the wounds are reopening again / we're blood brothers." So it's kind of bittersweet and very loving and, at the same time, very melancholic. It's a lot of very, very mixed emotions and, musically, there are a few Celtic nods.'

Elaborating on the song's deeper meanings, Steve Harris told journalist Johnny B, 'It touches on the dark side of your thoughts. It is also about feeling ashamed about what is happening in the world. It is about all these horrific things going on and people read about it in the paper but they just turn the page over, and the horror is ... well, muted. I am not saying it's forgotten because it might be on their minds but there's not really a lot they can do about it. It just kind of gets put to one side, and we hope somebody somewhere takes control and guides those who can do something about it.

'The lyrics are about all sorts of things. There are a lot of elements to it ... Basically it is saying that we are all made up of blood and tissue, and there is good and bad in the world, some people are unlucky in life ... things like that all rolled up into one ... It is very thematic.'

Turning to the album's first single, 'The Wicker Man', Dickinson told journalist Clay Marshall, 'It started off being a riff with Adrian. I thought it sounded very bouncy and I started putting a catchy little melody to it. I thought, "This could be a real good single," so we started playing around with it. Steve came in with some of the anthemic bits at the end. And there it was, four-and-a- half minutes long without even trying to get a single-length track. It was the song we wrote together – the first song the whole band actually rehearsed together.'

Lyrically, Dickinson told *Classic Rock*, the song was inspired by 'the Wicker Man of the cult 1970s movie,' adding to journalist Vinnie Apicella that 'the title comes from a reference in the song called, "The shadow of the wicker man is rising up again ..." in the lyric. We just lifted the title from that. Originally the song was going to be called "Your Time Will Come", which, of course, is the chorus.'

Dickinson also told Marshall, 'When I was writing the words to it, you start free-associating things. What happens to this kid? The first line in the song is, "The hand of fate is moving," and suddenly, "OK, out of bed. You – your turn today." The idea of the finger of fate knocks you to your feet, says, "OK, what'cha gonna do about it?" The dumb kid at the back of the class, who's always too shy to speak – his tongue was frozen – all of a sudden he pipes up. He goes, "Hey, I think you all suck!" He's got something to say. This whole thing – fly from the gates of dawn, eternity calling you his way. In the song he says goodbye to gravity, he says goodbye to death. Live for every moment. One of the lines in the song that just sums it up is, "Every second is a new spark to set the universe aflame." If you just take that attitude in your life – every second that's alive is another spark in eternity – it's great. It's a great, uplifting vibe.'

Elaborating further, the singer added, 'What I was trying to get on the lyrics was a feeling, just this real positive vibe – the same vibe I get when I stand on stage in front of all these people and they're all yelling at you, and chanting and singing with you. This huge, uplifting feeling: "It's just great to be alive," right at that moment in time. The song is totally in favour of promoting that attitude, that one day something good is going to happen to you and, when that day happens, don't back away from it. If you get an opportunity, grab it by the balls with both hands and just do it. Hence, "Your time will come." When the audience goes and sees Maiden, that's it – your time has come.'

Speaking to Vinnie Apicella, he added, 'It's catchy, it's got a huge anthemic chorus, it's got the big kick-ass guitar riff in the beginning ... so that's going to be the first single.'

On the subject of singles, Steve Harris told Johnny B, 'We thought as soon as we wrote it that it could be a good single with a good catchy chorus. We've had a lot of really good catchy choruses in the past as well but what do we really know about singles? We've released singles in the UK but they never really get played on the radio anywhere. Maybe we've been releasing the wrong songs as singles – who knows!

'Even if we release the right kind of song, whatever that is, would it do anything anyway? I don't think so probably. I mean, I don't think it really matters what we release as a single really. Sometimes I would just prefer to go the completely opposite way and release the bloody longest song on the album, basically saying, "Fuck you." I mean, they wouldn't play it even if it was three, four, five minutes long so they're not going to play something that is eleven minutes long, are they?'

Turning to the inspiration behind 'The Nomad', which featured what *Billboard* called 'Arabian-flavored contributions', Bruce Dickinson told *Classic Rock*, '*Carry On Follow That Camel* is what "Nomad" is! It's about the Bedouin, the warrior tribes of the desert. I don't think that there any great layers of hidden meaning to this other than what it's about. I mean, when Steve wrote songs about Alexander the Great, they were basically about Alexander the Great and that's it. The lyrics are basically there to tell you about nomads, and about how mysterious and strange they were, how they were pretty nifty and jolly fearful people, and that's what it is. The big picture is the effect that the song has. Well, it's not really a song. It's a nine-minute piece.'

Co-writer Steve Harris added that the track had 'a big *Lawrence of Arabia* type vibe. That is the sort of stuff I really like, the sort of stuff I get off on – film theme music. It is a big influence really. It always has been though so it's not as if we have gone off in a different direction. That is the sort of thing people *always* ask us when we start writing: whether we are gonna go off in a different direction or not. We don't go off in any direction – we play what we feel. We don't try and be this or that or let trends dictate to us.'

Elaborating further to Johnny B, Harris said, 'The theme of the music was great and this is what I was talking about before, where the vibe of the music sends us in the right direction for the lyrics. It was definitely one of those sorts of tracks. The vibe was very Middle Eastern and that is what inspired the lyrics. We were all thinking of the desert and stuff.'

Of 'Out on the Silent Planet', Bruce Dickinson told Ironmaiden.com that the song was 'a fairly straightforward romp through sci-fi territory and a sort of "Run to the Hills" revisited vibe – certainly by halfway through the song, 'cause I certainly wanted to get into the old gallop bit from the get-go and Steve was like, "Let's not give it to 'em straight away."'

Delving into his muses for the lyrics, Dickinson added to Clay Marshall that they included the 1956 movie *Forbidden*

Planet. 'Monsters from the Id – such a fabulous concept that I just wrote a lyric about a society ... In *Forbidden Planet* they discover a civilisation long dead but run extremely efficiently by these vast machines. The society itself has long since perished but the technical paraphernalia that they've constructed will last for ever. I kind of thought, "Well, that's nice," but took it a few stages back and thought, "If the society was dying – if it poisoned itself – would it seek to export its insanity elsewhere, out of the silent planet?' Hence the idea of a world which has poisoned itself with its own prosperity and its own gods. It created its own gods and its own gods destroyed it. That was what was in my head but that all comes down to about two lines in the song. I try to create a life for each song that makes sense to me. Then I'm happy about singing it.'

Dickinson added to the band's official website that, in the end, the song was about 'a bunch of aliens who have destroyed their planet, and now they've left their silent planet and they're coming to get us'.

Co-writer Steve Harris told rock journalist Shelly Harris that the song was an example of the band taking 'a different direction for some of the writing. Some of it was new for us as we wanted to try a few new and different things ... It definitely has a catchy chorus – well, two choruses really. It has a chorus and a sub-chorus. It had a feel about it when we were recording like when we did "The Evil That Men Do". That had a strong bridge, which could have been a chorus, and then you hit the real chorus, which takes you even higher.

'Bruce wrote the lyrics for that one ... Again the song has lots of different moods in it. The bits in the middle and the end are real favourites of mine.'

Turning to one of the album's longer cuts, 'Dream of Mirrors', Harris explained to Johnny B that the song was about 'the dark side of things. It's about people's thoughts and how they suffer from dreams and nightmares and all sorts. That was the main influence and source of material. I think dreams are so intriguing and you never really have an answer for them so, therefore, it is endless. I feel there are more songs than pictures about that sort of thing and I find it a fascinating subject.'

Bruce Dickinson enthused to *Classic Rock*, 'It's a cracking song. It's pretty lengthy. The chorus is fuckin' blinding! One of the best choruses I think Steve has ever written and one of the best lyrics he's ever written too. "I only dream in black and white." I mean, straight away fucking great! Shit, who dreams in black and white? Wow, do I? Is that weird? "I only dream in black and white / I only dream because I'm alive / I only dream in black and white / to save me from myself!" I was like, "Oh man, he's a tortured motherfucker, Steve is sometimes" – and he does have these dreams and déjà-vu things and out-of-body things going on for him.'

Discussing his muse for 'Ghost of the Navigator', real-life pilot Bruce Dickinson told Clay Marshall that the song began with 'a riff that Janick had and, when I listened to the riff, I just got the big picture of boats, storms, seas, a journey, a quest. I thought, "OK, that's good," and then I thought, "The quest. Vikings. Led Zeppelin. Weird, whoopy vocal things with a little bit of flanging on." Sort of vaguely taking it in a Led Zeppelin direction. The drum [track] has got that big, smashing, Bonzo-type feel to it. So there's a bit of the Zep element coming in on that track.'

Lyrically, Dickinson told *Classic Rock*, 'I thought about navigation. So, being a vaguely arty bloke on occasions, it struck me as a metaphor for life. So suddenly I had a plot for the song. It was a great big, epic sea-faring journey, and the journey was life and the navigator was us as we were writing it. Steve said, "That's a really cool middle bit and we can have this bit in it too," and I really liked it. I don't know if he was on the same wavelength as me but it sounds to me like a big storm 'cause I've already got the navigator lashed to the helm so as not to be tempted by the sirens on the rocks trying to distract him. Trying not to be distracted by all the ghosts of his subconscious, the ghosts of his failed aspirations, and also his own fears, that it may all be pointless when he gets there and he does it because he must. That's the only answer he can give.'

Discussing two of the album's deeper cuts, Dickinson told *Classic Rock* that 'The Mercenary' was 'a good solid track. Not a huge amount to say except that they're mercenaries and they're generally a bad thing. They're generally cruel and heartless fiends who cynically kill people for money. A fairly conventional tuneful Maiden rocker comparable to a sort of "Die With Your Boots On" type thing.'

Of 'The Thin Line Between Hate and Love' Dickinson said, 'It almost sounds like a UFO track in places. It was quite an unusual thing we did on the vocal on this, 'cause it's more of a hard-rock rhythm going down and we actually put a harmony on the entire verse. So it's quite an unusual sound for Maiden. It's basically about karma – in other words, what goes around comes around and you reap what you sow ... There's hope if you have done the right stuff, otherwise down you go to the pit of Hell!!'

Of 'Fallen Angel' Steve Harris told Johnny B that the song was 'all about Good versus Evil. To me, the whole song is musically influenced by Thin Lizzy. It has that Celtic vibe to it at the beginning that is very Lizzy. I think the song is very ... well, not commercial but the chorus hook is very catchy.'

Casting some light on its lyrical inspiration, Bruce Dickinson told *Classic Rock* that the song 'is about sort of being chosen as a human sacrifice so it's deep and dark. I think Steve was having a dark patch when he wrote the lyrics to that one. Steve's got a lot of dark patches on this record. Adrian wrote the basic song and it's got a pretty catchy little chorus. But I hope we don't have too many people flying out of windows if it's a single because the chorus is, "Could it be it's the end of the world / all the things that we cherish and love / Nothing left but to face this on my own / 'cause I am the chosen one." Aaaarrghh!!! People chucking themselves out of windows! Like in *The Omen*, where there were people hurling themselves out of windows, shouting, "Damiaa-a-a-n!"'

Turning finally to the album's title track, Dickinson told journalist Vinnie Apicella that the band 'had the album title first and then wrote the song. It's about a book, *Brave New World* by Aldous Huxley, and it's just my impression of the book ... It's an enigmatic kind of title and then I thought, "Well, seeing as it's going to be the album title, we better have a song. We wrote it ass backwards."

Delving more deeply into the meaning behind the lyrics, Dickinson added to journalist Marshall, 'The song is my take on the book or my take on one of the characters from the book – Savage. The book's kind of a tragedy. Other songs I start out generally with not necessarily books or films. Once I got the feeling of that song it was just a matter of free associating.

'In the song, "Say goodbye to gravity" – we've conquered gravity, we've conquered death. "Hello to eternity" – he's leaving for ever. Just all these ideas. "The ferryman wants his money" and you're not supposed to pay the ferryman because then you've had it; he's got your number. In this case, the guy does the other thing – the ferryman wants his money but you're not going to give it back. He steals money from the ferryman and says, "Hey, you push your own fucking boat." So he's walking out of Hell (laughs) – this guy's doing everything. That was the idea – the whole uplifting, anthemic vibe. You can do what you want on one day, which is a very May Day sort of spring theme, renewal and everything.

'I had the whole Maiden thing in mind when I wrote the song as a context. It was like, "This is what we're doing. We're bringing this monster back to life and we're breathing life back into everything that it touches, the audience, the album, everything." It was a good song to do first.'

With their songs down, the band turned to the monumentally important task of settling on a producer for their comeback

LP. Initially the thought crossed their mind to invite long-time producer Martin Birch – retired almost a decade – to return to the console but, as Bruce Dickinson firmly stated to *Classic Rock*, 'He's retired … He does not make records any more. He just does not do it.'

Dickinson added his concern that the recording medium had changed from analogue to digital in the time that Birch had been out of the game. 'This is quite a difficult thing to say because I love Martin. I have a huge amount of respect for him and he was my favourite producer bar none out of all my childhood – you know, growing up listening to records. But when you have been out of making records the way records are made nowadays and stuff like that, when you've not been involved, it can be very difficult to get back into it.

'And I am not sure Martin necessarily wants the stress that's involved. I think that was one of the major reasons he thought, "OK, enough's enough." Martin's been making great records all his life. He would like to finish his life at a ripe old age, rather than expire of a heart attack in some studio in LA. I also wouldn't like to go back with somebody just for the sake of nostalgia.'

Guitarist Janick Gers echoed in an interview with *Promethean Crusade* that 'Martin [Birch] doesn't want to do production any more. He's gone. I love Martin – he's done everything I've loved over the years but he don't want to do it any more so we're looking for fresh pastures and we're moving on.'

That process of moving on, Gers added, began with

'talking to a few different record companies and some major producers – three or four that we have in mind to do the album. We want to make an album with a major producer, and try to capture that essence of what this band's about because I don't think we've done it yet, production-wise. I think we feel that was one of the reasons, when we got together, to talk straight away about [needing] a producer to come in.'

In a conversation with Triple JJJ FM Radio he added, 'Steve was actually the first one to say, "I think we need to get a top-line producer in to do it," and I was like, "That's my question answered really," about people's commitment to making Maiden number one again.'

As they worked through the possibilities Steve Harris told journalist Johnny B that, when they got to Kevin Shirley's name, 'I had really liked the stuff he had done before and then, when we had a meeting with him, it was just the vibe and the way he does things, and the way he talks about stuff ... It was great. Obviously you all have to get on with the guy and we got on well with him when we met him so that was great as well. We have liked the work he has done before, like Silverchair ... He has worked on albums for loads of different bands and, more importantly, different types of bands, mainly still within the broad spectrum of rock, and we just thought he would be the right bloke for the job. I think we have made the right choice.'

Having said that, Harris acknowledged that he was 'a little worried about working with a different person you don't know. I always would be because you don't know what they're going to be like. Obviously you know what they've done work-wise and their reputation. We met him and he seemed like a nice guy. However, until you get down to it you don't know if you're going to click with somebody or not but it clicked perfectly. It's just the way he works. It's very similar to the way we've been working the last two or three albums anyway, in a lot of ways. There were some things that he was doing that we hadn't been doing before but it was really good working like that.'

Bruce Dickinson added to journalist Robert Jock, 'The reason we got around to using this guy was that he was the one producer who basically came up with the attitude that – well, we said, "What are you going to do with our sound?" And he said, "I'm not going to do anything with your sound. Your sound's great!" He said, "It's just that your sound has never sounded as good on record as it has live." He said, "I was there the other night and you sound great! So all I'm going to do is stick you in the studio and put mics in front of you, and let you do what you do best."'

That live-off-the-floor approach was one the band embraced with open arms, as Steve Harris told journalist Johnny B. 'Basically, we wanted to go in the studio and add all the vibes, all the freshness of coming off a tour and playing together again ... Well, this album we approached differently and we actually rehearsed for quite a while before going in and doing it ... This time we had a sort of on and off period, a sort of longer period to write. We were writing bits and pieces here and there then going in to finish off the writing, then basically rehearsing the songs at the end.

'Normally we just rehearse a song and then just do it as we're going along. It's just a different way of approaching it when we're recording at my studio, at home, as we haven't got a time problem there ... The recording and the rehearsals are all one and in the same place. Whereas you can't really go and start spending the same sort of money it would cost for the recording to just rehearse. It's just insane to rehearse for a month in a recording studio that is costing whatever a day – it's just stupid. So it just has to be a different approach.

'We rehearsed the stuff really well first so that, when we went in to do the backing tracks, they went down obviously a lot quicker. We'd rehearsed the songs as if we were going to play live ... We've done it that way before years ago and we enjoyed it, and it worked. Either way really it works because the end result is the same, in the sense that you just want to get the best performance down. Either way I like doing it – it doesn't matter one way or the other really.

Dick Bell, Maiden's production manager, found the band a venue to rehearse in, in Belgium. "It's just a really good place. [Belgium is] just a great place to rehearse, the people are nice and the whole atmosphere was relaxed and friendly ... It was just a really good size and sound. For me, it was just a good vibe there. Like I said, the people were friendly and stuff like that, and that means a lot ... You could just relax and nobody knew where we were. We weren't getting hassled by anybody and we could just go there, do a job and get on with it, basically. Conversely, that's also what's good when we rehearse at my place: I know nobody will bother us there. I know it was kinda out the way but it's good. Yeah, it was a great place.

'We have all worked in many different studios over the years but it is just when you have done three different albums at the same place ... it is just good timing to go and do something somewhere else.'

Trying out both a new studio and a new producer didn't change everything about Maiden's approach to the album. 'Maiden has never been in the situation where someone comes in and starts dictating what kind of songs we write,' Steve Harris added in the same interview. 'It's important to get someone in that wants to get the right sort of performance out of you. You don't want someone that wants to just change the songs around. We knew that he [Kevin Shirley] wasn't that type of guy or we wouldn't have entertained him.

'[A producer] influences the sound, obviously, to a certain degree. If we were doing sounds that he didn't like, he would say so. But yeah, he influences the sounds, the way you record – he's the engineer as well. He doesn't influence you in the writing of it. The right songs are already arranged and written beforehand anyway so he doesn't influence you like that. He might have odd ideas – it's the same with other producers we've worked with, like Martin Birch. They may have odd ideas but whether we used them or not is another thing. It depends whether you liked them or not.'

In a conversation with *Promethean Crusade* Janick Gers added, 'Iron Maiden have a sound. I think it needs tinkering with. We don't want to bring somebody in who brings their sound. A sound wouldn't be what it's about. We want somebody that can enhance the sound that we have. A major goal is to capture the sound we have live – with all the excitement and the aggression and the power and everything else that goes with it – on the record, which is very rare. If we can get someone to do that and we get the songs together that I think we have the ability to write, we're in for a cracking Iron Maiden record.'

When it came to fleshing out the album's arrangements, Bruce Dickinson said to *Promethean Crusade* that the band needed no outside input. 'We have more songwriting firepower than at any time in the band. The vibe within the band is just so on at the moment and I think it will remain so. This is the same kind of atmosphere that we had on *The Number of the Beast* – it really is. It really is that good. I think we can do the greatest Iron Maiden album there's ever been.

'We rehearsed it like crazy. I mean, it had to be tight, with all three guitarists in the same room making constant eye contact. We were surprised when we heard it all back, how tight the whole thing was.'

As always for mainstay Steve Harris, his greatest relief in the whole production process came early on. As he told Johnny B, 'When the writing stage is done, personally, so much of the pressure is off for me. If you know you have really, really strong songs – OK, you know that then you have to go in and record them and get great performances but, in a way, it is academic. I don't mean that lightly but it is academic in the sense that we *know* we can go in and do that. You know it will be hard work but you know you can do it.

'You can never know, though, that you can come up with great songs before you start recording and that is, for me personally, the most stressful thing. I have said many, many times that songs are the lifeblood of a band. If you have a bunch of great songs, you have half a chance of making it. If you believe you have great songs, it is irrelevant what others say and it shouldn't phase you. For example, you could have ten people in a pub choosing their greatest Maiden tracks but they will probably come up with a different ten than the pub down the road with a group of people trying to choose the same thing. Writing is the most important time.'

Once the band had wrapped pre-production Steve Harris recalled that they had no problem in moving to a new studio. 'We did *Fear of the Dark*, *X Factor* and *Virtual X1*, and we also did a bit of *No Prayer* there [Barnyard], although it wasn't properly in the studio, as we did it in the mobile studio. We also mixed a couple of live albums there as well. So we did quite a bit of stuff there and we just felt like it was time to go somewhere else really.

'It's the same as in the 1980s, when we did three albums in Compass Point in the Bahamas. We did the recording there, and then went and mixed the stuff in New York, at Electric Lady studios. We did that for three albums and it felt good to go somewhere else. So we did some other stuff, like *Somewhere in Time*, at Wisseloord Studios in Holland. Who knows whether we'll go back to that one or somewhere else?

'I mean, I really like the latest studio [William Tell in Paris]. The studio was great – great environment to work in and really enjoyable. Very well equipped. The people were really well on the button with professionalism and totally together. I was very impressed with the studio. I would work there again, definitely. Whether we'll do that next time round, who knows? That's not something we're thinking about yet. Whatever we decide now will probably change in a few weeks anyway – such is the nature of the beast.'

Bruce Dickinson added to journalist Clay Marshall that the transition from one studio to another was seamless because '[Producer Kevin Shirley] selected a great studio for us in Paris called William Tell, which enabled us to realise the idea of doing it live. [It had] a huge-sounding drum room, loads of glass so we could all get eye contact with each other while we were playing. At the same time, I could do my vocals completely live and just be separated from all the racket.

'We knew we were going to be doing it live so we rehearsed all the songs up, having come off the back of the tour. We wrote the songs before going on tour, left them not unfinished but unrehearsed, certainly, and then came back to them after the tour with this whole touring-head [mindset]. Then we rehearsed them as if we were gonna go and do a gig, and then we did a gig, basically, for each song but in the studio.'

This approach also meant, as Dickinson told journalist Vinnie Apicella, that the energy they generated on stage was reflected in the new LP. 'The attitude of the playing is so enthusiastic and raw on the album because we recorded the whole thing live and, therefore, the vocals are live, the guitars are all live ... Everything was done all in the same room at the same time: no guide tracks or bullshit like that. It was like playing onstage but in the studio.'

The singer added to MTV.com that this tactic had been favoured by the whole band. 'I think there was universal disenchantment with the idea of doing an album piecemeal on ProTools. Nobody wanted to indulge in that nonsense.'

When the time came for the band to begin tracking, Dickinson described to journalist Vinnie Apicella how 'Kevin walked in the first day in the recording studio having not heard a note of music! So he just said, "OK, guys, what are we going to start with today?" and we said, "Wicker Man." "Oh. Well, what does that sound like?" And by the end of the day he found out, 'cause it went down in one day – and all the rest of it went down in similar fashion. At the end of twelve days we'd recorded all the tracks. Kevin had no idea of what these songs were going to sound like until we started playing them for him ... As a producer, just the very concept of going in and recording the whole thing live, he enabled that to happen. First of all, he's got a great grasp of live recording.

Steve Harris added to journalist Johnny B, '[Kevin] has got a particular way of working and it works very well. His way is to go in and do songs one by one, rather than going through and doing, for example, rhythm guitars for all the songs bit by bit or song by song. We also do some vocals and bits and bobs of that particular song.'

Dickinson added to Marshall that the producer 'actually has a whole set of equipment that he brings with him into the studio, which enables each individual member of the band to get exactly their own mix. We have our own little eight-channel mixer by the side of each guy. It just turns what is normally a nightmare into a little dream machine.'

Harris also said of Shirley, 'When you're stuck in the studio for all that time together, you need to have fun. What I mean is that I'm the one that's in the studio with him every day, day in and day out. I am there more so than the others so I need to get on with him. We got on really well together. It is so important to have a good working relationship. I imagine that there can't be anything worse than going into a studio if you don't like the person that you're working with. We were really lucky because we all got on really well with him and we would definitely work with him again.'

The band's mainstay was equally as happy about working with Dickinson and guitarist Adrian Smith again. 'It's always worked. There is no big deal really. There was no déjà vu. Everyone has made a big deal out of the formation or reformation or whatever you wanna call it apart from us. We are all big enough and ugly enough to get into this, and do this without there being any problems.'

Citing the band's collective dedication to the process of recording, he said, 'At the end of the day, you still have to all go in and do the album in the way we make albums – you have to go in and do it in a studio. You still have to go in there and concentrate for a certain amount of hours a day, whether you are at home or away. Once you are in the studio it doesn't matter. It can be snowing outside or brilliant sunshine – you don't know as you have your head down in the studio.'

As they began recording Harris said that the band employed a strategy of 'working on each track as we were going along, getting the sounds we needed. That's what made mixing easier because we were building a track up layer by layer, one at a time. You just do bits and pieces – whatever is needed and whoever is available at the time. You just get them in to do bits and pieces, and that's how you carry on. You get a working format going. You have to be very strict in your procedures as you only have limited time.'

To handle the album's synthesiser parts the band brought in Geoff Bova to work alongside Steve Harris. In an interview with journalist Johnny B the bassist complimented the keyboardist for his willingness to tackle the job. 'When you are trying to cram it all in with three guitars, rhythm guitars, drums and stuff, it is very hard. There is a hell of a lot going on. It really is not easy to do.'

Elaborating on Bova's role, Harris added, 'Geoff is a guy that just sits there in his room, surrounded by all different keys and sounds, and he then takes them and layers them up. The layered version sounds really like an orchestra. I was really pleased with that. I was actually so pleased with how it turned out because I was a bit tentative when I sent out the tape to him as I wondered what on earth he was going to come up with. I was a little worried in case he went completely over the top but he actually came up with exactly what I wanted so I was well pleased. I had a vision of the direction I wanted to take the song in and the work he did fitted in great. I was very pleased.'

Citing some of the specific collaborations they felt were synthesiser stand-outs, Harris used 'The Nomad' as an example. 'He did a little bit on the middle section and, again, he did exactly what I wanted him to do. The rest of "The 'Nomad" – believe it or not – I actually played the keyboards. The main reason for that is because I know what I want and I know the timings I need. I could get Michael [Kenney] to do it but I think, by the time he has sat there and learned it and the timings, I might as well do it myself and save time and get exactly what I want.'

Turning to the gear used to record what *RevelationZ* magazine complimented as consistently inventive drumming, skins master Nicko McBrain told IronMaiden.com, 'I use a slightly smaller kit in the studio just because there will be two less microphones listening to the tubs. It helps to let the kit be a bit larger-sounding. Also I'm getting to that time in my life where it makes things a little easier. My kit consists of 9 toms, snare and bass drum – 6, 8, 10, 12, 13, 14, 15, 16, 18 floor, 14 x 5 snare, 24 x 18 bass drum. Paiste cymbals, 14 hats – 12, 16, 17, 19, 20, 24 power crashes, 20 medium crashes, 17, 18 rude, 22 china – all the Dimension line. I use DW foot pedals – one bass-drum pedal and one hi-hat. I only have one DW turbo pedal, mate, that's it, I can tell you.'

In sharing how he achieved the sheer power behind his drums, McBrain revealed, 'I use my left-hand stick back to front, as it gives me more weight and, therefore, more power for the snare hits ... I use primarily single-stroke rolls. I don't use two bass-drum pedals as I have never found one to be a problem. I am very happy to play the way that I do just now.' The result, according to Sonic Abuse.com, was 'Nicko's drums sounding better than ever', while iTunes.com said they had 'never kicked harder'.

When attention turned to co-producing the guitar triumvirate of Dave Murray, Adrian Smith and Janick Gers, Harris told Johnny B, 'There was always gonna be a different edge to a certain degree anyway with the fact we have three lead guitarists. That in itself I would have thought was not going to be an easy thing to handle.'

Kevin Shirley, he enthused, 'handled it brilliantly. Yeah, I do think he has given us an edge because it is just working with someone new and someone who is very positive, and he has a great vibe about him. He is a pleasure to work with – in fact, he is great fun to work with. When you are recording, that is what it should be about – fun! You should be enjoying recording. I know it will seem a weird thing to say as this is our twelfth studio album but, although I enjoy it, the studio is not my favourite place to be. I would rather be on stage so to be able to say I enjoyed it is important and to work with the right people is important.'

As for the guitarists themselves, Janick Gers told IronMaiden.com, 'The three guitars work very well together with the minimum amount of change to any of our styles. It really works quite naturally.'

In the same interview Dave Murray addressed the question of whether ego ever got in the way of divvying up leads by explaining it wasn't a problem. 'We split everything up. So there is a nice balance in the solo department.'

Recalling the group's tracking process as they worked song by song, Steve Harris said to Johnny B, 'We'd lay all the guitars down – the rhythm guitars, some overdub guitars – and they would all go and record them together, rather than do them individually. This system worked out great. However, again I think that was because we were so well rehearsed, we could do that. I think that, if you weren't as well rehearsed and you'd just gone in and done them as we usually do them, by taking each song at a time, it may have been different. It is, after all, just a different approach but the fact that we had rehearsed for a month beforehand meant that we could just do things like that – and easily. Everybody could just do their bits and it meant that we could just do it like that.'

As iTunes.com noted, 'Even as Smith rejoined, the band retained the services of his replacement [Janick Gers], giving a new thickness to the old band's trademark attack.' Gers agreed, telling Metal-Rules.com that, because of the three players, 'we have added a lot more to [the album]. On some of the songs we have detuned down to D on one guitar so it is the Maiden sound with a down-tuned D underneath it and it adds a little bit of fatness to it.

'We tried to add to the songs, rather than just do the same things. They are only subtle changes and only to make the band sound bigger and louder. Also some of the songs had more than two guitars and it meant we could play them live on the road, i.e. three-part harmony ... On some of them we are doing three-part harmonies and there are some solos where we are doing joint solos so it is kind of like what we would call in the studio an ADT, where you would have one solo on one side and another solo on the other side, and sometimes it is only a millisecond behind and it's kind of like double tracking. So we have done a bit of that. It has been very creative, what we have done.'

To stay consistent with what the *Guardian* called 'their galloping bass and dueling guitars formula', Steve Harris told IronMaiden.com, 'We have three guitars now but we layered some songs like that in the early days as well. It depends what the song needs.'

In sharing some specifics of how they achieved their individual sounds, Janick Gers began by explaining to IronMaiden.com, 'I'm just trying to make the songs better by penning a melodic yet aggressive solo or something that hits but can be a bit off the wall ... I think the sound for the solos is a bit dirtier and that is because the solos were mainly done live with the backing track as opposed to setting a sound up. But I felt the spontaneity was worth the slightly inferior sound quality.'

Of his gigantic volume he added, '[I plug] straight into the amp but turned up very loud. I also knock the pre-amp off a bit as I don't like it if it is too distorted. I like to hear the notes distinctly as opposed to fuzzed over.'

In the same conversation Dave Murray told IronMaiden.com about his effects board. 'The effects are from a JMP rack. Distortion, echo, flange, delay, wah. I know H [Adrian] used to play in D tune with Bruce.'

In different interviews Gers told of his excitement at having Bruce Dickinson back singing over the top of his axe mates and himself. 'Having Bruce back is brilliant,' he told Metal-Rules.com, 'and I feel we are on top of our game.' To *Promethean Crusade* he said that, for Maiden's sound ultimately to jive with his ear, 'I like things toppling over the edge into white noise but it comes back to melody ... I've got to like the singer ... and [Bruce] is one of the best singers there is.'

Amazingly, considering how lengthy and detailed the album's arrangements and time signatures were, Bruce Dickinson recalled to *Promethean Crusade*, 'We finished the back tracks and, therefore, virtually *all* the tracks within twelve days. Then we sat on our asses for the next six weeks while everybody went through in minute detail the six versions of each song and decided, "OK, this is going to be the master drum track. Now let's have a listen to all the guitars." Version one of the guitars, version two of the guitars and so on. That takes like a day for each song for each set of guitars so there's ten days. Then there's the vocals – each song, each six versions of the vocal is another day, so ten days of vocals.

'We worked five days a week with weekends off – that's four weeks. So two weeks to record everything live, four weeks to sort it all out, two weeks to mix it – there's eight weeks – and then two weeks to fool around with it and do overdubs and bullshit, and backing vocals. There you have a three-month album.'

When attention turned to mixing, Steve Harris told

journalist Johnny B that this was where Kevin Shirley came into his own. 'He is a superb mixing man without a doubt. That is just another reason why we wanted to use him. I learned a few little tricks from him. His expertise is great and we knew we wanted someone really competent. With three lead guitar players we knew it was gonna be tricky to say the least.'

Bruce Dickinson also paid tribute to Shirley's skills, telling journalist Vinnie Apicella, 'He's a very good mixer. I've never heard anybody mix so fast and so well and so confidently as Kevin. He understands rock 'n' roll ... He understands guitarists and what they like to hear. When he's copping a solo out of three or four different takes, he puts things together and musicians just love it! He's very quick and very sharp, and doesn't fuck around. He doesn't have you hanging around, trying to make you do something you don't want to do naturally.'

Listening back following the completion of tracks, Dickinson told Apicella, 'It's the best-sounding ... it's classic, vintage, whatever you want to call it. It's the Maiden sound that everybody wants to hear on this record. It's also the best-sounding version of Maiden there's ever been in terms of the production values and everything else.'

When it came to sequencing the album, Dickinson told *Intoxicated* e-zine that it was a daunting task. 'The whole album weighs in at sixty-eight minutes! So there are a lot of very long songs in there and so many great moments on the record. It's hard to single individual ones over and above anything else but ... I think "Blood Brothers" is a stand-out.

It's pretty different for Maiden. It's got a full-on sort of Celtic vibe – strings and the whole deal. That's pretty unique for Maiden. But there's a track called "Dream of Mirrors", which has got a drop-dead chorus and some great words. There's a load of great stuff on this record.'

Harris added to journalist Johnny B that, in the course of arriving at the final track listing, 'When we pan an album out we try to have light and shade. We had "Blood Brothers", which is a quiet at the beginning and end. We thought that "Mercenary" will bring the tempo back up again. We then thought that "Dream of Mirrors", which has those quiet sequences near the beginning, will slow the pace again.'

The band ultimately chose the album's opener, 'The Wicker Man', as their first single, a selection that iTunes.com hailed as 'definitive Maiden – a multi-part opus that is at once furious and violent and gloriously anthemic ... The immediacy and vitality of the playing is felt [throughout].' Bruce Dickinson told Vinnie Apicella that the band chose the song because 'It's catchy, it's got a huge anthemic chorus, it's got the big kick-ass guitar riff in the beginning ... Fuck, single ... radio cut... whatever. So that's going to be the first single.'

Released on 30 May 2000, Iron Maiden's comeback was an instant smash with fans and critics alike. *Metal Hammer* hailed the band for its 'prog-tinged melodic bombast'. Popmatters.com would say that the album embodied an 'energy that matches older records like *Piece of Mind* or *The Number of the Beast*'. Observing that *Brave New World* 'pretty much picked up right where the "classic" line-up had left off on 1988's *Seventh Son of a Seventh Son*', *Billboard* noted a return to form 'with a faithful rediscovery of Iron Maiden's best-loved sonic aesthetic and compositional quirks ... As comeback albums go, its excellence was undeniable, and announced ...only Iron Maiden's triumphant return.'

iTunes.com went further. 'More than a reunion, *Brave New World* is a renewal. Clearly, these six people were meant to play together and together they muster a power that is unparalleled, even in the excessively aggressive landscape of modern metal.' Popmatters.com agreed. 'The band found themselves completely rejuvenated when key members Bruce Dickinson and Adrian Smith returned to the fold.'

Acknowledging that the new record 'sounds uniformly strong', Bruce Dickinson told MTV.com, 'It's because of the uniform strength within the band.' In an interview with *Intoxicated* e-zine he added that the results of that camaraderie had produced an album packed with 'everything that Maiden fans will need! And maybe a little bit more than some of them expect ... I think we proved that with this record. A lot of bands get back together and what they deliver is certainly less than their best ... and this is Maiden at its absolute peak!'

In response to the BBC's hesitant note that 'Maiden are still Maiden, OK, but you can hear the influences that Bruce Dickinson's solo works have on the Maiden sound', the singer told the Disseminated Group that, through blending the two eras into one style, 'what I get out of Maiden is the pleasure of rediscovering my past and reinterpreting it again, and projecting it to a new audience with pride and with respect. Also I get a chance to completely reanimate us, this band and project to where it really rightfully belongs: right at the top of the pile again. And that is something I thought's really worthwhile doing.'

Released by Sony Records in the US and EMI throughout the rest of the waiting world, *Brave New World* returned the band to the Top 10 for the first time in years in the UK (No. 7). It also cracked the Top 40 of the *Billboard* Top 200 Album Chart – notable considering the band's final album with Blaze Bayley had sold only 84,987 copies in the US. There were new hits too: 'The Wicker Man' – which was nominated for a 2001 Grammy for Best Metal Performance – peaked at No. 9 on the UK singles chart and cracked the Top 20 of the *Billboard* Mainstream Rock Chart, and 'Out on the Silent Planet' reached No. 20 in the UK.

Embarking on their second world tour in two years, the revitalized band blazed through their classic catalogue along with the new hits, quickly reconquering the top spot of a genre they had helped to pioneer 20 years earlier. As a result, *Billboard* reported that fans worldwide 'saw the New Wave of British Heavy Metal legends commanding ... with the same unmitigated power and authority as they had during their mid-1980s heyday'.

The band's enduring yet evolving fan base tripped out guitarist Adrian Smith, who later told KNAC, 'When I came back into the band – I think it was 1999 or 2000 – I noticed there was this new set of fans, young kids coming to the shows. The first thing I noticed when I got onstage was these young kids up front because I was expecting people of that generation who grew up with us really, basically our age. I know, having kids myself, they're really into the artwork, the whole Eddie thing. That draws them in – the really young kids – and then they get into the music.

'There are probably a lot of fans, a lot of older fans, that are looking for something a little more alternative, something that's got more melody, guitar solos, more traditional – big, bombastic, like a big rock-show thing. And not many bands are doing that, only the older bands, and there's not really too many of them around doing what we do.'

That fan loyalty, Dickinson told MTV.com, was down to the fact that, 'when the band is on and we're doing it live, there's no other band on Earth that can touch us ... I really, really believe that. It's kind of a cool challenge as well because so many people have written the band off. A lot of the people who have written the band off were not really kind of experienced Maiden watchers or Maiden fans. They didn't really know how good the band was deep down.'

With the new album going gold in the US, Brazil, Canada, Germany, Poland, Sweden and the UK, Popmatters.com celebrated the fact that woven within the album's musical fabric was 'an unrivalled optimism that promises the group's continued performance together'. Indeed, as Rolling Stone Magazine would later report, in the aftermath of *Brave New*

World's release, 'the revived, Dickinson-fronted Maiden went on to have a second successful career, releasing another string of charting albums'.

CHAPTER THIRTEEN

DANCE OF DEATH (2003)

'2003's *Dance of Death* marked the triumphant return of old-school Iron Maiden'
iTunes.com

'The time with Blaze is just a side of the Maiden history. It was a different experience but having Bruce back is just as it's meant to be' Nicko McBrain

As the Millennium began to shape in the context of popular musical trends metal was surging through a comeback based on both the momentum of Maiden in and of itself as a metal force, making them one of the hardest-working – and most in-demand – metal bands in the business. As Popmatters.com reported following the return of the 'two prodigal members [Bruce Dickinson and Adrian Smith] back into the fold in 1999, the band – a sextet for the first time – staged a highly successful comeback tour in support of *Ed Hunter*, a compilation [supposedly voted for by the fans], which also formed the soundtrack to the computer game of the same name. In 2000 *Brave New World* proved there was still plenty of gas in the tank.

'Then there was the huge world tour, culminating in a performance in front of a quarter-million insane Brazilians in Rio de Janeiro in January 2001, which was recorded for both a double live album and a DVD release.' (*Rock in Rio*, which reached No. 1 in the UK and No. 2 in the US DVD charts). The band also released another successful DVD (the video compilation *Visions of the Beast*), their third best-of album (*Edward the Great*) and a lavish box set of rare recordings (*Eddie's Archive*). And there followed yet another triumphant tour of Europe and North America.

Reflecting on the band's legacy now that it was approaching the 30-year mark, *Stylus* magazine argued that without Maiden there would be 'no Swedish melodic death metal – and thus no modern metalcore. No Maiden, no power metal (e.g. Dragonforce, Hammerfall and so on). Any heavy band with twin harmony guitar leads owes a debt to Iron Maiden. Black Sabbath may have patented the tritone but Iron Maiden made melody a permanent part of metal.'

As the band headed into pre-production on their 13th studio LP Steve Harris explained to the Rock Brigade website that, as always, 'we allow ourselves a six-week writing period and that's all we do. We don't write on the road so we just go in with new, fresh ideas.'

Guitarist Adrian Smith added to *Rock On*, 'We don't write all together. Personally, I always have an idea or two, which I write down, then Bruce comes along and adds something and so on ... Dave, Janick and me tried composing together but we ended up playing ten-minute solos on guitar! I wrote enough, like Steve and Bruce.'

Musically, drummer Nicko McBrain explained to Metalfan.nl, 'We present our ideas and we work them out.

Usually with Steve, we work out our parts first and then the rest of the band comes in.'

As for his own compositional process, Harris told Rock Brigade.com that, when writing, 'I play a lot of bass chords and stuff. I'm not too analytical about my own playing, I just write the songs. I'm more concerned with what's good for the song than with what I'm playing. Which is probably why I've been playing less of a role lately because that's the way the songwriting has been. That's what's needed. The songwriting always depends on what's needed or not needed.'

Lyrically, Harris added in the album's liner notes, 'I tend to conjure up imagery within my own mind when I write.'

While drummer Nicko McBrain insisted to Metalfan.nl that 'on *Dance of Death* we go back to our roots', Bruce Dickinson told *Rock On* that the expanded line-up's songwriting had been strengthened by the fact that 'we've been working together for over three years and now that shows in our compositions'.

In describing the overarching conceptual theme to the album, guitarist Janick Gers explained to Finnish metalhead journalists Luxi Lahtinen and Marko Syrjälä that, while 'there are eleven separate songs on *Dance of Death* ... there is also a common theme here through the album as well, which has this certain type of a connection through each song there too'.

In a full-band discussion on the musical inspirations behind the album's 11 tracks, Adrian Smith began with opener 'Wildest Dreams', pointing out that it's 'not one of our nine-minute jobs so it fits well with our older, classic stuff'.

Guitarist Dave Murray recalled of 'Rainmaker', 'I had a few riffs and some chord progressions all worked out, and then Steve added some melodies to it before Bruce wrote the lyrics. I remember Bruce saying in the rehearsal studio one day that the intro riffs inspired him to think of raindrops and that's where the rainmaker concept sprung from. In fact, you could almost see the light bulb going off in his head as he thought about it – it was very inspiring.'

Of 'Montsegur', another mediaeval battle epic that iTunes hailed as 'a brutal, melodic assault that recalls the group's glory days and showcases lead singer Bruce Dickinson at his venom-spitting best', the singer told *Rock On* that it was 'was written by Janick ... It has a heavier sound and a dark atmosphere.' Warming to the topic, he added, 'Given the nature of Iron Maiden, in terms of the sounds that we make and the songs that we do – and we do make a fair bit of racket when it comes to loud riffs – songs about mediaeval battle and massive slaughter are a bit of a given ... But really, there is so much great stuff and so many great stories throughout history that you can make parallels with the modern day, particularly when history repeats itself as often as it does, that it makes for some very colourful subject matter.

'The way I look at it is that, if you're going to plunder something for the lyrical basis of a song, at least plunder something that has really happened, rather than invent some crass sword-and-dorkery epic.'

Turning to the title track, 'Dance of Death', Janick Gers said that the song had been inspired by the old black-and-white Ingmar Bergman film *Seventh Seal*. 'It depicts a knight searching for reasons to live. What struck me was that he was looking around the world for something worth surviving and fighting for but, when the Death character finally came to claim him, the knight still wanted to survive long enough to find some faith and humanity in this world of plagued wars. The knight begs Death to let him live long enough to find his faith and hope but, in order to make that bargain, Death plays chess with him for his soul. In the end, Death comes for the knight and his troops anyway. It's an allegorical tale but it's fascinating.'

The guitarist added that 'right at the end of the movie, when all the actors had finished filming and gone home, Ingmar Berman edited in a sequence which no one knew about, when the camera backs off to the horizon, where all these distant people on mountains are dancing to a tune and it's the so-called "Dance of Death". For a long time I thought of incorporating that image somewhere into the song. Steve took that concept but went somewhere else with it completely to come up with some amazingly visual lyrics.'

Of his contribution Harris said, 'A lot of our songs ... have dark moods and are full of drama and I love all that epic film stuff. When you're searching for inspiration for lyrics, sometimes you do look toward certain sources like movies or books and, with the type of music that Maiden make, the moodier or the darker [the] subject matter the better!'

Clearly proud of the results, Gers said in the record's liner notes, 'A lot of bands just can't do songs like that any more or, more likely, they just won't allow themselves the freedom to do songs like that, which is a shame.'

Turning to 'Paschendale,' Adrian Smith – the song's primary composer – recalled that 'the music almost wrote itself and really suggested the theme for the song. While writing, I could hear the different parts echoing the differing parts of the battle. A frantic part had to be about the conflict and another, more relaxed section would definitely represent the calm before the storm or a lull before a counter attack.

'[The song] is classic proggy Maiden territory for sure but it's an area which I hadn't ever really attempted to write before. People usually associate me with our more commercial material, like "Wasted Years" and "Two Minutes to Midnight", but I thought I'd have to go at writing a Maiden epic. And five days later I was still there writing it!

'I remember going to a library to get lyrical ideas and the very first book I saw was on the battle. The title alone just captured my imagination. I gave the music to Steve and I explained where it was coming from and what I thought it should be about, and he was off writing the lyrics.'

The finished product gave lead singer Bruce Dickinson chills from the opening notes. 'It's got a little guitar riff in the beginning – not the big heavy one but a little plaintive one. When I was in Army cadets at school, we used to go out on night exercises and they'd fire these parachute flares and star shells that would go up into the sky, emitting an eerie, ghostly light as they twinkled and illuminated before falling back down. That eerie, twinkling sound that the flares made is the exact same sound of that small riff at the beginning of the song. As soon as I heard it shivers shot down my spine and I just knew it was going to be amazing.'

Producer Kevin Shirley added that, when the band first played him the song, it resonated 'with the majesty of battle but it also manages to convey a sense of poignancy over the magnitude of loss and the sheer pointless of it all'.

Of 'Journeyman', Bruce Dickinson said that as he and Harris worked on the song, 'lyrically, I had images of somebody making decisions with his heart regardless of where it was going to lead him in life'. As a consequence, the song is 'about the journey you're on through the whole of your life, and the chances that you have to make your choices and decisions. You can choose to rot away slowly or you can choose to go and do something mad and glorious – it's all up to you.'

Musically, he added, '"Journeyman" started off as a chorus, which we initially thought would turn into a big anthem affair. Then, when we got our heads around it, we wondered what exactly we were going to do with it because, if we'd turned it into "Born in the USA", it was just going to sound crass. So instead we got quite trippy and dreamy with the verse and it worked.'

Turning to 'Face in the Sand', Dickinson revealed in the album liner notes that the song was 'about modern world propaganda. It's about how we all think that we're so damn clever and how we imagine the things that we build to be timeless but, in reality, they still fade away in the end.'

In the same notes he commented of the idea behind 'Age of Innocence' that the band was not trying to be political. 'Maiden don't do that. This is just a personal view only but I think what I'm saying is what a lot of people are thinking. If you take the law into your own hands, they come down on you like a ton of bricks for being a vigilante so I guess I'm letting my anger and frustrations out as an Englishman who doesn't feel safe any more.'

'New Frontier' was something of a surprise, in that it was the first song that drummer Nicko McBrain had ever presented to the band as the primary composer. 'It took him twenty years to write a song so no wonder it's so good!' quipped Steve Harris. Adrian Smith added to *Rock On*, 'Our surprise is Nicko! He had some very good ideas. The thing many people don't know is that he plays very good bass and he wrote the basic guitar riff of "New Frontier".'

Admitting to Maidenfan.nl, 'Of course I was nervous,' the drummer added, 'I had the lyrics and melodies all worked out but I took it to Adrian, and we worked on the bridge and the chorus together.' Next he showed the parts to Bruce. 'He worked a little bit on them because it wasn't running that well. I didn't mind if it fitted better for him because I'm not difficult when it comes to that. Adrian also fixed the solos.'

Even with all that work on it, McBrain confessed he still hadn't faced 'the most nerve-wracking part', which was 'when it came to me playing the melody on the bass for three guitarists to show them how I felt the song should go. After that, of course, you graduate to having to play it to Steve. He strapped on the black acoustic bass and he's like, "Go on then, show me what you've done." [I'd got] halfway through it and he's like, "'Ere, that ain't half bad, Nick. Do you wanna play the bass on the song when we record it?" So I think that was a compliment he paid me.'

In the end, Harris was proud to include the song on the record, saying in the album's liner notes, 'The bottom line is that it's a great song. If it wasn't, it wouldn't be on the album. "New Frontier" is really catchy and it's different to what we might have done otherwise so Nicko bringing it in made it a more interesting and varied album.'

Moving on to the band's decision to work once again with producer Kevin Shirley, Harris felt that, as with the previous album, 'working with Kevin again in the studio was great and the second time around was better because we didn't have to go through the BS of having to get to know each other. We knew what each other wanted. With Martin Birch there were a lot of similarities. They both have a great sense of humour. Their overall professionalism was about the same.'

Shirley added that, in many ways, working with the band was the easiest gig he'd had as a record producer because 'They're Iron Maiden, I'm not Iron Maiden and all this great music is coming from them. All I do is bring the best out of them. So all I really want from anyone listening to *Dance of Death* is to understand and appreciate that this is Iron Maiden being as pure as they can possibly be. That'll make me a happy man!'

Guitarist Janick Gers told *Rock On* that, among Shirley's other talents, the band enjoyed his navigating the pitfalls offered by digital recording. 'Nowadays ... the simplicity of the past doesn't exist ... There is more digital equipment and Kevin knows how to use [it] very skilfully. You see many people working with the mix – it's like working with an atomic bomb and you have to know exactly what to do so it doesn't blow up ...

'[Also], the thing that Martin Birch had managed was to avoid having a sound as a producer. He didn't bring the sound of Deep Purple, Wishbone Ash or Black Sabbath in Iron Maiden. In contrast, what "Mutt" Lange did with Def Leppard and Bryan Adams was to have his signature on the sound. Kevin had succeeded in what we wanted – he makes the band sound like Iron Maiden and doesn't try to make us sound like something of his.'

Heading into recording, which began in late 2002 at Sarm West Studios (a converted church in Notting Hill, London), the band was chasing a sound that the BBC would later celebrate for its 'almost organic feel', with the rhythm section of drummer Nicko McBrain and bass player Steve Harris 'providing a rock-solid backing' for the three guitarists' 'fretboard fury' and Bruce Dickinson's 'operatic yowls'.

Explaining that, from the band's perspective, they were seeking to capture the energy of a concert for the record, Janick Gers told journalists Luxi Lahtinen and Marko Syrjälä, 'We went on without a click track or anything like that and we just recorded this album live, where we are our best. Because of that this album has a live sound ... It moves, it breathes and it sounds just great, I think.

'It's that kind of thing that many bands don't do at the

moment because they are playing with the click tracks, which keep everybody like ... Uh, how should I explain it? Their songs simply don't breathe too much and, if you go back and listen to bands like Led Zeppelin and all those old bands, you can feel that the thing is moving a little bit. Now people go and say, "That's moving!" but I think that's great because things like that should move and breathe a little bit.'
In an interview with *Rock On* he concluded that, ultimately, 'the thing Kevin has managed is to make us sound like when we are playing live'.

Nicko McBrain echoed these sentiments in a conversation with Maidenfan.nl about the impact of this approach on the drum sound. 'We don't use a lot modern techniques to record. We recorded the drums [in] analogue and then we put it on a hard disk. On the previous album we immediately recorded that digitally. *Brave New World* was more drum orientated and the guitars are relatively quiet. Now it's the other way around. The drums are still present put they are quieter. Almost no overdubs, a few solos, some singing and that's it.'

Offering fans some insight into his powerful style, the drummer revealed to *Metal Masters* that the secret to his sound revolved around 'a lot of practice and playing time. Also it depends on what the bass line is laying down. The more intense it is, the more you have to play on the foot. It just comes from a lot of playing. One of the most important things to be aware of is your balance. By this I mean how you sit behind the kit in relation to the distance from the bass drum and the height from the floor. I sit very low and my upper leg is parallel to the floor. I only use the side of my big toe on the bass drum pedal. You should find what works best for you.

'[For my] fast double-bass drum, it sounds like a double bass. I should have used two pedals because it's so fast. But I have to confess that I used two pedals on one song. I had to 'cause the fast piece is very long and I couldn't keep it up with one foot.'

Turning to the specifics of the Premier Series kit he played during tracking, McBrain revealed that his kit was comprised of 6, 10, 12, 13, 14, 15 and 16-inch toms, an 8-inch floor tom, a 24 x 18 bass drum, a 5½ x 14 Modern Classic snare and Paiste signature cymbals – the same set-up for live work and in the studio.

Turning to the album's elaborate stacks of layered guitar parts, Dave Murray explained to Tim Cashmere of the Australian magazine *Undercover* that finalising the elaborate arrangements was 'a very natural process. We sat down and worked [it] out ... You know there's a lot of details to work on but basically, having three guitar players, it really moulds together very well. It can sound like one big guitar or it can sound like three individual guitars. It depends what piece of music we're playing at the time but we get on well together and it's a very natural environment, you know? There's different ways of playing things on a guitar so we kind of do it so it moulds together and sounds like one unit, if you like.'

In his conversation with journalists Luxi Lahtinen and Marko Syrjälä, Janick Gers added that, while the process should be made simpler by the fact that 'everyone from the three guitar players in this band could be the main guitarist of the band', it was also made difficult by that fact. 'Our intention is to make the band sound better with the three guitar players and that's a challenge. Sometimes you simply don't have to play because you just don't need to put too many guitars on some parts. We don't want to destroy our songs with too-big guitar walls and ... I mean, I don't know if there is anything that difficult in here. We know how well we all are playing and we know that we do our best. So, when you come up with some ideas you believe in, you're trying to get it to sound great – the best sound you can get.'

To get the best blends on each song, as Gers revealed to *Rock On*, 'We don't tend to show off our playing abilities. I believe that each one of us could easily stand as the only guitarist in a big band. There is no competition as to who will be the best guitarist in the band but as to how we will combine our abilities better so that we can make the songs sound better ... We try to come up with different ideas to make our compositions better ... Musically, we make the songs better without trying to stick out so many times we play simpler but the collage of the three of us gives the better result.'

Dave Murray added to *Undercover* that, towards the end of that sonic collage, 'We do do a lot of harmony guitars and we do do a lot of unisons but it's kind of going back to our influences as well. A lot of bands, like Thin Lizzy and Wishbone Ash ... used harmony guitars and so we've kind of taken that concept really and added it into our own unique way of playing. With each song there may be a harmony guitar or unison but it's basically whatever fits the song, but we just like to take full advantage of it. Hey, you've got three guitars so it's just doing as much as you can, you know?

'Also, it's a thing where you want to complement that particular song so we wouldn't just do it just for the sake of doing it. It's there just to enhance a particular melody or like a musical statement to that piece of music. I think it's fun and it sounds very musical, and now with three guitars we can do three-guitar part harmonies, which we've actually used on some of the tracks. Other times there would be unisons or there'll be one guitar playing melody. Basically we have ample ammunition to do what we want. We've got a lot of ammo there!'

Offering fans an inside look at the band's top-line gear used in recording the guitar parts, Murray said in the same conversation, 'Janick, Adrian and myself, we all use Stratocasters with the Marshall amps. You know the JCM series with the built-in effects you see? They're like 200 Watt amps and stuff so, with Maiden material, it's not just straight-ahead big chords. There are a lot of slow passages when you need that clean sound as well so basically those amps are very versatile. Also the Fender Strats are very versatile guitars as well so all three of us use Strats anyway. We're like the old purists really so it's like Strats and Marshalls but we're using more of the clean stuff as well as the heavy stuff.'

Discussing the LP's only acoustic song, the closer 'Journey Man', drummer Nicko McBrain recalled to Maidenfan.nl that the band decided to try something new. 'First we had the normal version, with electric guitars and normal drums, then I said we should use an acoustic version too ... I used bundle sticks, which look like a brush. It gives a very different sound but it fits the style well. The number turned out great. It was the first time we did something like that ... It was a real great experience to play a song like that.'

'We've kind of used acoustics a little bit in the past,' Dave Murray added to *Undercover*, 'but I think Adrian, Steve and Bruce came up with the idea for that song ... It actually sounds so much better being all acoustic. We're still using some keys and synths in that particular song as well but we thought, "Let's do something a little bit different." We have actually never done an acoustic track ever so we thought, "Let's give it a go," and I think it's a real haunting melody, and it's really beautiful lyrics and stuff. It's really sweet and I think, with acoustics, it just gives it another variation.

'It's a pretty full-on, heavy album with a lot going on, and then you come to the very last track and it's like, "Wow!" It just brings you down. It takes you out of the album in a nice way, you know? I love acoustic stuff and it's great to be able to do it with this band and on this particular album. I think it's just a timing thing – Maiden felt we were ready to put out an all-acoustic track on an album.'

Talking about the record's sometimes lush orchestral arrangements, Nicko McBrain told Maidenfan.nl, 'I'll let you into a secret – it's all done with synths.'

As Murray explained to *Undercover*, 'We use keyboards on this album quite a bit but we use them in orchestration-types of scenarios, like having a keyboard sound like a violin or cello or something ... We've been using keys and stuff on quite a few of the albums but this is probably the most we've ever pulled that rabbit out of the hat there. We've used it quite extensively on a lot of the songs but a lot of it is quite a wash, and it just adds a bit more colour and a bit more weight to a particular piece of a song. We'd use anything – if it sounds good, we'd use it.

'It just seems, having the orchestration and using the keyboards and synths to do that, it just makes it sound bigger and fatter, and gives a more dynamic sound to it all but, if you strip everything away, the songs are strong enough to stand out by themselves. You just want to enhance a piece of music and make it sound the best it can sound so, if you want to use keys to add a particular effect to a song, I think it's good! To me, there are no rules in music. If it sounds good to your ear and if it sounds good musically, you can use a set of bagpipes if you want – whatever makes that song sound its best.'

Elaborating, Murray explained to *Rock Brigade*, 'Even when you start an album and the songs are coming together, you really don't know what shape it's taking until everything's down. It just happens naturally. We don't force the issue.'

As recording wound down McBrain recalled to Maidenfan.nl, 'In the early days, when we finished a song, we would go to the pub and celebrate. Now we only do that when we are finished with all the songs. Otherwise we wouldn't have the time to record an album!'

Steve Harris shared with Rock Brigade his feeling that, as

mixing got underway, this album took on a 'darker and a little more theatrical' sound than the band's past few LPs.

Highlighting some of the other directional differences the band had taken musically on their latest outing, Bruce Dickinson revealed to *Rock On*, 'From the first four songs there's a breath of fresh air within the band. I believe that everybody is very satisfied with what we have accomplished. I don't know how it manages to sound so Maiden while having all these new elements.'

Agreeing, McBrain offered his own conclusion to Maidenfan.nl. 'There will be something for everybody. People who are new to Maiden will find something to their taste and people who liked *Iron Maiden* and *Killers* will find something to their liking too. That number [that] reminds me of *Piece of Mind*, it wasn't done intentionally. It just worked out that way. There are a few short songs that last about four to five minutes – for Maiden standards, that's short. I think everybody will be satisfied 'cause the album has something for everyone.'

Dickinson was happy to credit producer Kevin Shirley with helping the band strike the right balance between making their classic vibe sound current without changing the band's sound. As he told *Rock On*, 'Kevin is very talented and, once again, he managed to raise the album's quality level,' adding that, while 'the future will show if we "glue" with Kevin like we [did] with Martin ... at this moment I'd say it looks like it'.

When it came to selecting an album title, Janick Gers recounted to journalists Luxi Lahtinen & Marko Syrjälä that, as before, it had been an evolutionary process. 'When we got together, we got a feeling of the album and then you kind of put the ideas down, and that title could be a good description [of] what this album is all about and where we are now. And at the end of the day, you can feel in your mind that we have chosen a really good album title for this album.

'There is a song there called "Dance of Death" and it tells about kind of a dance of death, lyrically. The initiatory surrounding of the song is about a guy who is kind of a storyteller. It's kind of a very long song, quite deep, about somebody who ... well, when you hear this particular atmosphere [that] is surrounding that song, you know where the ideas came from for the album and it does have nice ring in it too.'

On its release on 8 September 2003 Iron Maiden's new LP danced its way into the Top 10 of the UK album chart (peaking at No. 2) and the Top 20 of the *Billboard* Top 200 Album Chart. It went to produce two UK Top 20 hits, 'Wildest Dreams' (No. 6) and 'Rainmaker' (No. 13), with the former also reaching No. 11 in the US.

The BBC concluded that *Dance of Death* was 'a triumphant return to form for these heavy-metal legends' and assured fans that 'they won't have one dissatisfied customer'. As Popmatters.com observed, the band's 'trademark style of epic song lengths, orchestral riffs, powerful vocal melodies and galloping rhythms is far from the coolest thing in contemporary music these days but it's a tried-and-true formula that still works. And as bassist/primary songwriter/ fearless leader Steve Harris knows all too well, if it ain't broke, don't fix it.'

Billboard echoed this sentiment with their own observation that 'the group's innate ability to consistently cater to its fans' stubborn tastes, while maintaining a level of integrity that other veteran bands displace with unintentional Spinal Tap zeal, is a testament to its talent and experience'.

Embarking on the Dance of Death World Tour following the album's release, Iron Maiden would play before more than 750,000 fans over 50 dates across North America, South America, Europe and Japan in the autumn and early spring of 2003/04. More popular than ever with their legions of loyal fans, as well as a new generation they were gaining as their latest wave of success continued to rise, Iron Maiden were on top of the metal world.

CHAPTER FOURTEEN

A MATTER OF LIFE AND DEATH (2006)

'There have been only a couple of occasions in my career when the ENTIRE process of recording felt so complete – and it is on display here'
Producer Kevin Shirley

Heading into 2006's *A Matter of Life and Death*, Iron Maiden were back at the top of their game. The six-piece line-up now had two studio LPs under its belt and, as KNAC noted, 'Every disc they put out just gets better and better.'

Harnessing the power of the band's three-guitar assault, coupled with lead singer Bruce Dickinson's soaring vocal attack, Maiden's new studio LP was as electric as ever in both its pure metal power and its rejuvenating celebration of the band's sound itself as one of the cornerstones of the heavy-metal genre they had helped to not only prop up but elevate, LP after LP, over the years.

When the band regrouped after time off following their 2005 Eddie Rips Up the World tour the previous summer, they approached writing for the new album, according to a familiar routine. As guitarist Dave Murray recalled to LiveDaily.com,

'Steve and Bruce write all the lyrics and then the rest of the guys come up with the music. Steve will kind of be the nucleus so everyone collaborates with him. With ideas, everyone individually goes to Steve and he kind of knocks them into shape. Eventually, people will go to Steve and show them what they've got. Sometimes they're good as they are. We kind of work like that.

'Before we go into rehearsal the song will basically be there in acoustic form. Once we get with the band it really starts to come into shape. It's a little seed and everything grows out of that. It's a very natural process. Nothing is really forced. No one is bashing their head against the wall. The guys have really got some strong ideas. We want to keep it fresh.'

Steve Harris explained to journalist Steve Purcell that, while 'we allow ourselves six weeks ... the writing tends to be done in the first two weeks or so', adding, 'When I work on it with Adrian [Smith], it comes together in the first couple days really.'

In a conversation with *Ultimate Guitar*, Bruce Dickinson added that, after 'we wrote some of the songs ... everyone went away and had a think about their own parts individually and then we went into rehearsals'. In all, he said, 'it was three weeks to write it, three weeks to rehearse it'.

'We allow ourselves a six-week writing period to give us enough pressure to bring it out,' Steve Harris confirmed. 'We write a batch of songs and they come out as they come out.' That period and process gave the band enough time to achieve the 'high standards for what we want to achieve'.

Going into more detail on the rehearsals, which acted as

part two of pre-production as the band fleshed out the arrangements and added other rounding-out components to their new compositions, Dickinson recalled the band's routine. 'Every day we'd start with a rough tape and at the end of the day we had a song written, run through, maybe some of the words finished, maybe not [completely] finished ... but we had the melodies and the arrangement. And then the next day we did a different song.'

As the band wrote, Dickinson told *Ultimate Guitar*, they weren't intending to craft a concept album. 'But that doesn't mean that some of the subjects in the album aren't related. They are related but they're related by the fact that we live in the world that we live in. So, yes, there's a lot of songs about war, there's a lot of songs about religion and things of that nature because, when we look at the world outside us, that's what's going on at the moment. There's lots of fear and paranoia about life and death, and religion and war, and things like that.'

KNAC singled out 'These Colours Don't Run' as one of the album's stand-out cuts, praising its time changes and intricate solos as it told 'the story of the life of a solider in any time, in any war'. Delving into the inspiration behind the song, Bruce Dickinson offered to *Kerrang!* that it was 'an effort to put a human face on people who go out and fight wars. They call it "peacekeeping" but these people put themselves in harm's way and, whether or not you agree with the reasons why they're doing it, they're just doing their job.'

The singer added to MTV.com that the song 'confronts patriotism in times of combat. There's a business of soldiering and it has always run the same way, no matter what war we're talking about. It's guys whose fathers and grandfathers were soldiers, and some father is kissing his family goodbye and going off to war, and no one knows if he's going to come back in six months alive or in a body bag.'

Producer Kevin Shirley found Harris and Dickinson's lyrics to be 'compelling, deep and questioning', adding in an interview with Love-It-Loud.com, 'No one really tells *Maiden* to change what they do, which they do unlike anyone else in the world!'

'Brighter Than a Thousand Suns', Dickinson told *Kerrang!* was inspired by the atom bomb. 'The scientist that saw the first bomb go off said it was brighter than a thousand suns. The idea that human beings could bring about their own total destruction totally changed the way people thought.'

Guitarist Dave Murray offered to LiveDaily, of the musical side of composing the album, 'There's a lot of moods with these songs. They're not just straight-ahead bang, bang, bang. There's quite a lot of quiet passages and where it changes tempos. When we were making the album, we just had a really good vibe in the studio. We just felt each track was telling a story.

'The way we rehearsed and recorded, it felt really natural to play. A lot of stuff on this album, there's a lot of musical kind of tricky bits. The music is so strong with the melodies.'

At Sarm West Studios, Bruce Dickinson recalled, it was a seamless process transitioning from rehearsing into recording, quite simply because there was no separation between the two. 'We rehearsed, learned each song and then, by the time we got to the end of three weeks, we just managed to learn all the songs, just managed to get through every song. Then we'd sort of forgotten the first one but we had it on tape so we went straight into the studio the first day and went, "Hey, let's listen to the tape. OK, it's coming back now." Play it two or three times. Right, start recording. And that's how we recorded the album – each song at a time.'

That approach suited producer Kevin Shirley just fine. As he recalled to Love-It-Loud.com, it allowed him 'to get the energy of the raw band and the original studio tracking performance down on tape, and build from there. I'm mostly not a "let's-build-it-from-drums-up' kinda guy."'

'We don't get together to make records that much any more,' Dickinson added in a conversation with MTV.com of the atmosphere throughout recording. 'When we finally did, we were really excited and that excitement turned into this really productive period ... In the past we may have been a bit more uptight but we're all just seriously relaxed and chilled about things now, so we're able to work well together and not get worked up ... Ideas were just buzzing through the air, and everybody was listening to each other and feeding off the energy.'

Capturing that energy, for producer Kevin Shirley, began with tracking Steve Harris's bass. That, the producer explained, 'anchors the sound – it's the armour of the beast and Nicko's big thumping groove is the heartbeat of the beast!'

In an interview with NorthJersey.com, drummer McBrain offered his own feedback on the rhythm tracks he and Harris had laid down. There was, he enthused, 'so much diversity on the new album. We've got a couple tracks that are pretty progressive, we've got high- and low-tempo songs ... I'm very proud of it.'

When attention turned to capturing guitar sounds, producer Shirley recalled in the album's liner notes, 'Janick would come in and listen to playbacks, and say, "I'm listening to all three guitars as one instrument. I'm not picking out the individual parts or sounds because three guitars is different from two and they all work as one instrument in Maiden.'

Elaborating on the individual elements of that blend which gave Maiden such a distinct sound, the producer added that, during recording, the three guitar players would bring 'their special chemistry' into the studio. 'Davey's playing is the best I have heard from him – fluid, melodic ... there's no one like him. In contrast, Adrian is razor sharp, blistering precise ... and in the mix Janick throws some madness – the stuff that's outside the box, as he's always looking for a way to be dangerous.'

Describing the specifics of his rig during tracking, Dave Murray told *Guitarist* magazine, 'I was using 50-Watt Marshall amps so it was basically a straight sound but I had this Pete Cornish pedal board with an MXR Phase 90 and Distortion Plus. We're kind of going back to that kind of minimalism now. We've gone full circle to a more pure tone.'

When it came to recording the lead vocals, producer Shirley revealed in the album's liner notes that they were all 'tracked live with the band and are the backbone of the songs', adding that he felt Dickinson's voice sounded 'louder and stronger than ever'.

For his part, the singer told *Ultimate Guitar*, 'When I came back to Maiden, I was a very different singer to the guy that I was when I left. Having worked with a lot of different musicians, having done solo records – in particular, *The Chemical Wedding* – I really expanded my range, not just vocally but in terms of songwriting. And I brought that back, I think, into Maiden and each album, I think, we've been moving towards really interesting territory. *Brave New World* was good as far as it went. It didn't step into any really, really new territory. And then *Dance of Death* – yup, we tried a few things on *Dance of Death*. Some of them worked, some of them didn't work quite so [well] but, you know what? It gave us the confidence to do this album and this album, I think, is really special.'

The singer went on to say that, in contrast to the band's last album, which he termed 'a kind of preparation, stepping stone, if you like, towards this album', he felt 'this album has so much more than "*Dance of Death*" – and actually more than almost any other Iron Maiden record. There's a depth to some of the songs and there's depth of feeling to some of the lyrics on this album that I don't think we've managed to achieve for a long, long time.

'We've tried with other records but this one, it's just – I mean, if you listen to a song like, say, "Out of the Shadows", there's nothing about that song which sounds like we were making an effort to sound like that. It just sounds natural, and it's clear and natural. And so much of the album sounds like that. When it's getting complicated, it doesn't get out of control – it keeps the power. The intros, they are "folky" but without being kind of embarrassing. Everything is just pitched in the right place and it's very rare that that happens. And it all happened very quickly.'

Indeed, Bruce Dickinson would reflect to MTV that 'we haven't worked that fast since we did *The Number of the Beast* and *Piece of Mind* in the early days and, back then, we didn't have a choice ... We recorded the album in three weeks ... and were just having a great time, writing really good music and then all of a sudden we were like, "Wow, we're done!"'

Echoing the singer's sentiments, Kevin Shirley recalled, 'We spent two months in the studio, from Go to Whoa, from Nicko's tubs up to the final mixes ... That's a tiny gestation period for an album because we lived life around it too.' In an interview with Love-It-Loud.com the producer added that, at the end of the day, his job felt like a breeze because 'Iron Maiden are who they are. I just record it and make subtle adjustments after the fact – fixes and tweaks and mix it.'

After Kevin Shirley and Steve Harris had finished mixing the album Harris made a decision not to go ahead with mastering the record. As he told *Aquarian Weekly*, 'When you work in digital format and you've got your mixes sounding just how you want, you don't really need a great deal of tweaking. Well, we don't. Some artists might but we don't ... When things are tweaked, they affect everything across the board and it tends to mess with the mixes ...

Because they're dynamic enough anyway in the mixes we don't really want anything messing with it. We did try different things, different frequencies and this and that. But it didn't sound better really. Sounded different but it wasn't better.'

As they had the mixes precisely where they wanted them by the time Harris and Shirley had finished, the producer shared via his official web blog that, '[Steve] has decided against mastering the Iron Maiden album and I'm quite pleased about that, although I did like the mastering job we did in [New York City]. It means that you will get to hear the new album exactly as it sounded in the studio, no added EQ, compression, analogue widening, etc. and I must say I am pretty happy with the end result. I think some tracks could use a smidge more top end and others a bump of bottom – but I know [Steve] well enough now to know how wary of outsiders he is and I fully expected he may have done that so I made sure I was happy with the results when I printed the mixes in the studio.'

Listening back to the record following its completion, Bruce Dickinson commented to *Ultimate Guitar*, 'I think this is one of the finest Maiden albums we've ever done. I'm really proud of it. I think, sound-wise, it's probably the best album we've ever recorded. Obviously I'm a huge fan of Martin Birch and his work with us but – you know, I think this is just a great-sounding record and I don't think we've done as good as this, ever.'

Dickinson added to MTV.com of the album itself that the band was 'still getting to grips' with it. 'It really is tremendously deep. There's a huge amount of stuff on it because we just didn't see any point in trying to make an album that was just like all the others. There are lots of bands making albums with five-minute pop-metal songs so we thought, "Let's do something really extraordinary."'

Drummer Nicko McBrain was equally dazzled, telling Musicradar.com that *A Matter of Life and Death* was 'a very adventurous record'.

Indeed, critics and fans alike were as wowed as the band was. *Brave Words/Bloody Knuckles* hailing the record as 'the strongest Maiden album in twenty years', while Blogcritics.com's reviewer was inspired to declare that 'the latest Iron Maiden album [has] ... reinvigorated my interest in the band and it has given me hope that older metal bands can age with some class and intelligence'.

The band's live-off-the-floor approach, the BBC's said, 'manages to preserve the raw element of a live performance because, as with their other albums, the band recorded *A Matter...* together in the same studio as live. Every song provides evidence that the band feed off each other and share a common energy.' iTunes.com concurred, noting that 'recorded live in the studio ... the whole record is a loosely knit song cycle with war at its core ... [The band] exhume prog-rock complexity and discipline, yet manage to bristle with the kind of small-club intensity usually reserved for acts half their age.'

Complimenting the band for 'their uncanny ability to write great lyrics' and 'wrapped around guitar orchestration that rock fans crave', the BBC noted that, with *A Matter of Life or Death*, 'the quality bar is raised once more'. It singled out 'For the Greater Good of God' and 'The Longest Day' for praise. The latter, it said, was 'outstanding with the partnership of guitar, bass and drums (and now even keys) flowing and developing throughout, while "Lord of Light" is one of those epic tracks destined to be listened to again and again – each time giving something new'.

KNAC.com also praised 'For the Greater Good of God' as 'a musical monster that clocks in at almost nine and a half minutes. Multiple time changes, very impressive, very flowing.'

As word of mouth quickly spread the band's first-week global record sales reflected just how far their star had re-ascended into the upper tier of living-legend, heavy-metal superstars. Blabbermouth.net reported that, following its retail debut on 26 August 2006, *A Matter of Life or Death* was 'on track to sell about 60,000 copies in the United States in its first week of release – significantly more than the 40,000 first-week tally registered by its predecessor, 2003's *Dance of Death* (which landed at No. 18 on the *Billboard* 200 chart), and that of *Brave New World*, which moved 38,000 copies in June 2000 to land at No. 39 on the *Billboard* 200 chart.'

The enthusiasm of the band's American fan base was repeated in other countries. The band's first-week charting positions made impressive reading: Sweden – No. 1, Finland – No. 1, Italy – No. 1, Germany – No. 1, Czech Republic – No. 1, Switzerland – No. 2, Norway – No. 2, UK – No. 4, Spain – No. 4, Ireland – No. 5, France – No. 5, Poland – No. 6, Netherlands – No. 7, Australia – No. 12, New Zealand – No. 34, Canada – No. 2 and the United States No. 9.

The band was elated and appreciative of the success, thanking their fans via the band's official website. 'In just the first week the new album has shipped over a million copies worldwide and impacted on the charts pretty well everywhere in the world!' In an interview with LiveDaily.com, Dave Murray pointed proudly to the band's success in breaking into the Top 10 of the *Billboard* Top 200 Album Chart as 'I think the ... highest entry we've had ever in the US. Also throughout Europe: it was No. 1 in nine different countries. For some reason, it's gone through the roof sales-wise in the first few weeks of release. It's quite incredible that Iron Maiden fans are out there looking out for it!'

CHAPTER FIFTEEN

THE FINAL FRONTIER (2010)

'It's the big epics on *The Final Frontier* that really illuminate the blazing fire at the heart of the band's creative core' *Classic Rock*

'Maiden have never been bigger and it's all been on their own terms' The BBC

'Once the writing's done, you feel this massive pressure cloud go away'
Steve Harris

By 2010 Iron Maiden had ruled the metal universe for the better part of 30 years, outlasting and outselling most of their contemporaries with close to 80 million records moved around the globe. According to *Brave Words/Bloody Knuckles* magazine, that had made them 'more popular than ever and globally revered in a way that no other metal band has ever come close to achieving, let alone sustaining for three decades'.

The cumulative impact of the band's catalogue across sub-genres of metal was in no doubt either as they headlined numerous stadium metal festivals around the world, drawing crowds in the tens of thousands who knew every lyric to every song and sang them night after night back to the band from a stage some argued they would never headline so popularly at that point in their career.

Popmatters.com argued that the band had been able to maintain such a track record of consistency because, 'in the ten years that have passed [since Bruce Dickinson rejoined], Iron Maiden's trajectory has skyrocketed simply because the band has refused to compromise ... The music is vital, it's continually challenging the band and their fans and, from a metal perspective, it's incredibly relevant.'

Such vaulting success brought its own pressures, however. How could the band maintain such standards? 'As metal moments go,' the BBC noted, 'they don't get much bigger than the arrival of a new Iron Maiden album. Expectations are always huge.'

As guitarist Adrian Smith admitted to Blabbermouth.net heading into recording their latest creation, 'There's always a bit of pressure to follow up the last album [but] in a way, it's good because it motivates you. We never get complacent: we always try our best for our own sake as much as anything else. As far as pressure for another album [goes], we just do what we do. We've been doing it long enough now; we know what we're doing.'

Indeed, the band had their alchemy down to such a science that, as Bruce Dickinson recalled to *Kerrang!* the album was completed in record time – despite the fact that 'this was the least prepared we'd ever been before we went into the studio. The groundwork came together pretty sharpish. We only spent two weeks in Paris.'

Drummer Nicko McBrain added to Music Radar.com, 'I would say my first and foremost goal was to finish the record without keeling over dead! In all seriousness though, we rehearsed seven tracks in Paris before we went to record them. Three of the other ones we had the sketches for but we had to work them up once we got in the studio.'

Talking about when principal writing for any Maiden album begins, Steve Harris admitted to *The Aquarian Weekly*, 'It's almost like going through a weird stage when you're doing it because you do feel sort of an anxiety. I can't really sleep properly when I'm writing. Too many ideas flying about all over the place so I don't really sleep very well.'

In describing the band's songwriting routine, Harris put such pressure into context. 'We don't allow ourselves too long because, if you allow yourself six months to write, you'll take six months. So we tend to put ourselves under a bit of pressure. And it is a bit of pressure; I certainly feel it anyway ... Not rushed – it just makes you feel a bit anxious because you know you've got to come up with good stuff. But that's always been a good thing; it's always been a positive thing ... A little black cloud goes away when you know you've got enough songs and you've got good material.'

In the same conversation Harris revealed, 'There's no fixed plan of who's writing with who or anything like that. It just worked out this time as well as the last album that I wrote more stuff with Adrian, purely because we were the first ones to get together really and it just sort of stemmed from there. It doesn't always work like that and it probably won't necessarily work like that in the future.

'It's just about getting really good songs and whatever combination of writers does that. We don't write twenty songs and use ten. There are always lots of bits and pieces flying around but basically we just use whatever we think is strong at the time ... Once we've got enough songs we stop. We've always done that because there's no point in really working on stuff that you can't record. We don't really give ourselves enough time to do that and we don't want to do that. We just want to record an album and go on tour with it.'

Of finalising the songs before to heading into the studio, drummer Nicko McBrain added to Music Radar.com, 'In terms of figuring out the progressions on the album, it was very much like it was in the old days. It was us together in one room going, "OK, how are we going to get from this bit to that bit?" It was natural, a band working as one. We were all looking at one another and communicating, and feeling at home, if you like.'

Once Iron Maiden's personalised Boeing 757-23A had landed in the Bahamas and the band settled once again into Compass Point to begin recording, guitarist Dave Murray recalled to *Billboard* that 'we breezed through the album really ... We were getting down a track a day – all playing together as a band, Bruce singing, all in the same room so there's a very live-in-the-studio feel to it. Once we finished a track we'd jump straight into doing some extra guitar bits. It was very quick for us.'

Producer Kevin Shirley – who *Classic Rock* magazine complimented for his 'vibrant production' on the album –

recalled on his web blog that 'Bruce Dickinson flew in for a few days and sang all his parts before flying off to the four corners of the globe, and Steve Harris stayed behind to finish the record with me. He's pretty hands on like that. Adrian Smith dropped in from time to time to hear stuff and, like in any band, not everyone has the same end result in mind but we get there.'

Using the same blog from his website Caveman Productions, Shirley added that the band's efficient recording routine was possible primarily due to how down to earth they were. 'I will tell you that Iron Maiden are the best band in the world to work for – it's a family and they are the most grounded guys I have ever met in this business. Nary a Ferrari in sight.'

Moving from the general to some of the particular tracks on the album, Nicko McBrain revealed to Music Radar.com that the epic 'When the Wild Wind Blows' was one of the three tracks the band hadn't worked up in pre-production. As a result, it was arranged on the spot in the studio but, even so, it proved to be an exceptional track. 'When Steve brought the song in, he showed it to us, gave the guitarists the chord progressions and everything. I could tell right off it was something special. Because of the kind of song it is, I said, "What do you want from the drums, busy or straight?" And he said, "Let's have it straight. We need some real groove on this track." That's all he needed to say. I told him, "Let me have what you're playing on the bass," and we worked that part out. Then we went for the second part, then we had the segue breakdown and it went from there.

'When we finished recording the song, I turned to Steven and said, "Next to 'Hallowed Be Thy Name', I think this is the best song you've ever written.' And he went, "Nahhh!" And I said, "To me it is." That's how I feel – I think it's just immense.'

When the band went to record the track, Dave Murray recalled to *Billboard* that playing the song's rhythm was 'a little bit different from what we've done before and there's lots of melodies ... It's a big song. We learned it in sections just because it was such a complex arrangement but it sounds quite natural [on the record].'

Nicko McBrain added to Music Radar.com, 'The funny thing is, there wasn't a lot of preparation for that song or any of the other ones really. It was just learn it, feel it and play it. That's what we did on this record. It was true to its form without a lot of contrived pieces. And there are even a couple of mistakes on it, to boot, which I think is great.'

Turning to the creation of the album's first single, 'El Dorado', its writer Steve Harris said, 'It's about greed and drawing people in basically – imploring them to do whatever and giving them the once-over afterwards. It's about that, loosely.'

Of the title cut 'The Final Frontier', Bruce Dickinson quipped to *Kerrang!* 'People will think it's a Trekkie type thing, won't they? We knew when we picked it that it would wind a few people up. I actually came up with the title before we'd written any songs.'

As Popmatters.com would observe in its review of the album, 'more emphasis is placed on ... [bassist] Harris and drummer Nicko McBrain. Consequently, the bottom end of this album is massive, the robust tone hammering home even more just how powerful this band still is.'

Sharing some of the specifics of how that power was harnessed, drummer Nicko McBrain told MusicRadar.com, 'Through the years I've found the only thing that really works is matching what Harry Harris plays. What I play on the bass drum is pretty much determined by the bass lines.

'As far as double bass-sounding patterns, I do have one little trick: once I've got the bass drum really kickin', I'll move my foot down the pedal about two-thirds of the way. To me, that's the optimal fulcrum point and I can get maximum results with less exertion. There is a problem with that, however, when you're trying to do a dynamic on a beat, particularly on a sixteenth-note group, you've got to really kick it. It's harder to do an accent when your foot's all the way down the pedal.'

In describing the finished album to *Billboard*, Dave Murray said *The Final Frontier* offered fans a mix 'straight-ahead, up-tempo rock songs with good grooves with some other tracks that are kind of longer and more complex.'

Nicko McBrain was more specific in talking to Music Radar.com. He felt that the new album marked 'a real breakthrough for us. It's filled with epic songs but it doesn't just go on and on for the sake of it. There's ideas and real heart on it. We felt everything we were playing. That's what makes a band a real band and a record a real record – the amount of feeling you put into what you do ... We took a lot of our history and revisited it in certain ways ... way beyond anything we've ever done before. The segues, the song structures, the time signatures – we placed no restrictions on ourselves ... I'm real proud to say we've still got that attitude; in fact, we have it more than ever.'

Steve Harris summed up his feelings about what the band had achieved in an interview with *The Aquarian Weekly*. 'I think it's a very interesting album. It's quite diverse and there's a lot going on. It's a long album, [an] hour and a quarter, so it's a lot of music. And, hopefully, people will like it. I think it's a pretty rich darn album – it's pretty different, I think.'

On its release on 13 August 2010 the critics went simply mad for the results. The BBC hailed *The Final Frontier* as 'a remarkable achievement from the metal titans' and reflected that Iron Maiden were 'truly living their purpose'. *Kerrang!* concluded that 30 years into their recorded history the band had pulled off 'a record that will still bowl you over in a decade's time', while *Brave Words/Bloody Knuckles* added that the band's 15th album was 'a stunning piece of work that expands on the band's recent progressive explorations, takes them into new textural and melodic areas and does new and intriguing things with that instantly recognisable compositional formula'.

That formula, *Classic Rock* proclaimed, produced results that were both 'bold and startling ... beautifully placed and disarmingly complex'. 'What impresses here are the complicated arrangements,' said *Rolling Stone*, while the BBC agreed that they were 'woven together beautifully'. Not to be outdone, *Metal Hammer* added that they 'repeatedly take the Brit-metal legends into uncharted territory. This is a demanding album but one that most Maiden fans are going to absolutely adore.'

The epic 'When the Wild Wind Blows' was singled out for particular praise. *Classic Rock* declared that it 'brilliantly evokes the mundane horror of Raymond Briggs' celebrated apocalypse tale with a series of grim but gripping twists and turns, delicate melodic gear-changes and enough atmosphere to sink one of Bruce Dickinson's beloved jumbo jets'.

Brave Words/Bloody Knuckles, meanwhile, applauded Steve Harris's composition 'from the opening seconds to a beautifully pitched denouement', observing that the track 'contains enough familiar traits during its deceptively smart eleven-minute duration to provide a link with the past while still pushing Maiden forward into atmospheric and harmonic territory that is as new to the band as it will be to the fans'.

Metal Hammer, for its part, hailed the opus 'as musically fascinating and lyrically brave as anything the band have recorded. Densely layered and uncompromising, this one will take a few listens to sink in but there is an insane amount of atmosphere and countless inspired melodic touches on display here. A stunning finale.'

The magazine also singled out 'Coming Home'. While conceding it was 'undeniably sentimental', it noted approvingly, 'This is plainly Bruce Dickinson's song, as he sings about returning home and seeing the lights on the runway as his plane descends to Earth. Not many bands could pull this off without setting off the cheese alarm. Maiden do it brilliantly.'

Even EMI were moved to issue a press release saying they were 'proud of their thirty-year career-long involvement with Iron Maiden' and trumpeting the astonishing first-week global success of *The Final Frontier*. 'In addition to the phenomenal number of No. 1 debuts in all parts of the world, Maiden are currently No. 2 in Australia, Belgium and Holland, No. 3 in Ireland Poland and Turkey, No. 4 in the US and No. 5 in Singapore. The debut at No. 4 on the *Billboard* chart in the US is the band's highest ever chart position.'

The statement went on to give an astonishing list of chart positions achieved across the globe by the album: 'No. 1 – Arabia, Austria, Brazil, Bulgaria, Canada, Chile, Croatia, Czech Republic, Denmark, France, Germany, Finland, Japan, Mexico, New Zealand, Norway, Portugal, Spain, Sweden, Switzerland, UK; No. 2 – Australia, Belgium, Holland; No. 3 – Ireland, Poland, Turkey; No. 4 – USA; and No. 5 – Singapore.'

In closing its review of the album, *Kerrang!* offered this celebratory toast: 'LONG MAY the Maiden REIGN!' adding, 'We're unbelievably lucky that they're still around ...'

The band's fans arguably felt the same, as did Maiden's members, all of whom had taken a roller-coaster ride through greatest commercial peaks and valleys of a genre they helped not only to found but also to pioneer and shape into the many generations that had followed between 1980 and 2010. Looking towards the future, Maiden sat once again in the privileged position of a band who had earned enough creative and commercial capital to head in any direction they wished without worrying about being in demand among fans quite simply because, as lead singer Bruce Dickinson reasoned in an early 2011 interview with the *Daily News*, 'The world needs Iron Maiden ...'

CHAPTER SIXTEEN

EDDIE THE HEAD

'His demonic face has stared maniacally from the cover of every Iron Maiden album since they released their first LP in 1980' CNN

'Eddie is larger than life' Guitarist Dave Murray

'Eddie was my invention' Artist Derek Riggs

Every legendary rock or metal band has its signature logo. Aerosmith have their wings; Motorhead the war pig; KISS the infamous tongue; and AC/DC the lightning bolt. For Iron Maiden, it's a cyborg named Eddie the Head.

Some would argue that Eddie is as much a part of Maiden's appeal as the band's music itself. CNN even went so far as to say, 'Edward T. Head, better known as Eddie, [has] morphed into the most recognised member of the band ... His demonic face has stared maniacally from the cover of every Iron Maiden album since they released their first LP in 1980.' On another important level, *Storytelling Magazine* noted that Eddie 'transformed Iron Maiden into a merchandising giant. The attraction to Eddie is as strong today as it was with his first appearance in 1979.'

Steve Harris told *Classic Albums* that Eddie, by design,

'can be whatever you want him to be – that's the cool thing about him. And that's one of the reasons we've always had him on the covers – it means we don't have to be. And it means we can do so much with him, all the things we don't want to do. I wish he could do interviews! Maybe one day, you never know.'

Delving back into Eddie's history, we arrive deep inside the mind of artist Derek Riggs. Telling fans a bit about his professional background, Riggs recalled to 89.8FM host Andy Lee that, prior to meeting up with the Maiden camp, 'I was painting all sorts of things. Disco covers, jazz, selling the odd portrait ... I did some jazz covers at EMI ... They started up a new label called Harvest Fusion, which lasted for about two albums before they knocked it on the head ... I did the covers for those. Kind of weird, surreal things that weren't painted very well ... because they wouldn't give me enough time to do it. Story of my life ...

'[One day] I was sitting alone in my shed trying to get my painting together. I was doing a lot of work on Symbolism – reading a lot of books, trying to work out what it was all about ... Reading a lot of horror books too because I'm sick and twisted inside [laughs]. There was an idea that H.P. Lovecraft came up with that you can make things more horrible by putting them up in your own environment, rather than sticking it out in Transylvania or somewhere. It was in the late 1970s and punk was big – there was this "wasted youth" concept going around: "We've all been thrown on the dustbin ... Help, we're dying now ..."'

To capture that spirit visually, Riggs explained, 'I designed this character with punky hair and I thought, I'll put a corpse in a T-shirt because I had a picture from the 1960s of this dead American's head stuck on a Vietnamese tank. That's what they said it was but it may not be true ... Anyway, I painted this head with punk hair on ... and stuck it up where I used to live. I used to walk a lot at night and I came upon this wall, which was all yellow because it had street lights above it and the moon was out too, which was kind of blue-ish looking. It was quite a stunning contrast ... so I used it. You get a feeling when something is right. I knew Eddie was right. He just had that look.'

Expanding on that look, Riggs told *Enough* fanzine, 'I made Eddie as the end result of learning to create symbols with pictures. I was studying Symbolism and how to make picture that could be read – pictures that could get a concept across. I was painting in a surreal kind of way, not in a horror style at all. Eddie was created in the late 1970s during the punk-rock boom and he was made as a symbol of the ideas of the time that the youth were being wasted by society. Eddie works because I did it properly and people identified with him. I never started out to draw scary stuff – that's just the way that one picture turned out to look and I got kind of stuck with it. Sometimes I think God is taking the piss.'

Talking to CNN about Eddie's features, the artist recalled, 'I wanted to paint a picture of a decaying, semi-skeletal figure in the streets of London. I needed some source material to draw from because I didn't really know how a human head decays. Then I remembered a photo collage I had done in the 1970s, when I was at school. Part of it was a photograph of a decaying head. It came from *Time* magazine and it was captioned as being an American soldier's head, which had been stuck on to a Vietnamese tank. Many years later I found the same picture in a collection of *Time* photos. There it was captioned as being an English soldier's head stuck on to a Nazi tank so now I kind of doubt that it was anything but a bit of war propaganda.

'Anyway, I used that picture as reference for painting the monster's head. Eddie was not inspired by the photo: I used the photo as reference for the painting. The painting was inspired by the English punk-rock movement in the late 1970s. They had this kind of street philosophy about the youth of the time being wasted and thrown on to the garbage. It was an attempt to depict that idea visually.'

Talking about what made his work different, Riggs told Horrornews.net, 'I wanted to make a monster that was actually a bit scary and not like all the other monsters that were around in the late 1970s, basically monkeys with wings. For reference I went back to a photo I had seen of a dried-up skull stuck on a tank and for the city background I used the part of London where I lived at the time – Finsbury Park – [which was] a bit run-down and decrepit. There is a story going around on the internet that this picture was the inspiration for Eddie. This is not true. The inspiration was to make a scary monster – I just used the photo as a reference for the look of the skin.'

On finishing his masterpiece, Riggs recalled being struck by an immediate instinct that he'd struck gold. As he quipped to CNN, 'As soon as I had finished painting the first picture of Eddie I sat back in the chair and thought, "That picture is going to make me rich and famous."'

On shopping Eddie around, however, he found the exact opposite. 'I showed the picture to my artist's agent, who gave it back to me with a grimace and said, "We don't think that picture is very commercial." I started showing my portfolio to the art directors of record companies, who usually drew back in horror as soon as they saw it.

'One time an art director threw me out of his office because he didn't think it was a proper rock-album cover. He pointed to a picture on the wall, which was his idea of a rock-album cover – it was an airbrush drawing of a waitress in a short skirt bending over so you could see her knickers. Another record-company art director suggested I go and get my hair cut and paint more normal things because I looked "like a weirdo or a mental case" and I shouldn't go around painting things like that, and I should get therapy.

'The picture was unclaimed for a year and a half before Maiden asked to see my portfolio. I gathered things together and thought whether I should take it along as well because it had caused me nothing but grief so far. I kind of thought, "Oh well," and stuck it in anyway.'

And so Riggs' determination to bring Eddie to life eventually paid off, as the artist recalled to *Lollipop* online magazine. 'The art director at EMI had some of my work on his wall and Rod Smallwood, Iron Maiden's manager, saw them and liked them. He was looking for an artist with a strange style and he took a shine to those not-very-good-but-rather-distinctive jazz covers. He asked to see my portfolio so I stuffed a bunch of paintings into this big wooden portfolio and dragged it down to the recording studio, where they were putting together their first album.'

Perhaps feeling the stars were lining up right not just for himself and Eddie but also for Iron Maiden's type of music, the artist explained to 89.8FM host Andy Lee that, at the time, 'Heavy metal had been the most unpopular from of entertainment in the universe for about five years and it was just starting to make a comeback. He had this band and he knew he wanted illustrated covers.'

Of the fateful meeting that would change everything, Riggs added, 'I went down to Wessex recording studios, where they were making lots of noise, and they were all there ... I had put lots of things in there and Steve Harris said, "Well, I don't want pictures of metal women.' I had this weird comic-book science-fiction stuff in there. I was always playing around with different styles – every painting seems to have a slightly different style. I wish I had a style – it would make life so much easier! [laughs] Anyway, they liked [Eddie] and they said, "Give it some more hair and we'll have that."'

Naming Eddie was actually a collaborative effort, as Riggs recalled in his interview with Lee. 'He wasn't called Eddie then. In fact, he was called Electric Matthew. [The picture] was called *Electric Matthew Says Hello*. I used give my pictures stupid names. If you went round to sci-fi conventions you would see pictures called *The Last of the Few* and '*The Few of the Many*'.

Elaborating to Lollipop on Electric Matthew's evolution in Eddie, the artist said, 'He didn't have long hair at the time –

he had punky hair because it was the late 1970s, when punk was going on ... He had the skull face and the lights in his eyes, and they used just his head for the logo. [Maiden] called it Ed because they just had his head – like, "We just got *'is 'ed.*" So that was that.'

Before Eddie made his debut, however, Riggs recalled to Horrornews.net that 'the original design had a punky look with a mohawk haircut but then, when they saw it, they asked me to make the hair longer at the back. At first it was OK – they left me to do pretty much what I wanted as long as it fitted the basic direction.'

Once they had the final image Riggs told *Lollipop*, 'The first thing that was released was a single, just before the first album. It was for "Running Free" and they wanted something sinister lurking in the background but they didn't want to give the face away. Then came the "Sanctuary" single, with the picture of Eddie with a knife hanging over Margaret Thatcher's body lying on the ground. She was called The Iron Woman because she was fucking up England's economy quite extensively. And there was another single called "Women in Uniform" that had Margaret Thatcher in military gear, and Eddie and two women.'

Controversy followed almost immediately although, years later, Riggs would tell Ytsejam.com that much of 'the flack for that single [Margaret Thatcher being knifed by Eddie, from the song lyric "Never killed a woman before but I know how it feels"] was invented by the band's management. They "banned" it – put the black square over her face and then showed it to the press and cried, "Censorship!" but there really wasn't any. The flack was all imaginary and self-generated for publicity. It's an old trick and it nearly always sells records – go and ask all the rappers who swear on their records all the time. If it depressed the record's sales, they would soon stop doing it.'

Following the success of Iron Maiden's debut album, Riggs recalled, to his relief, that 'the merchandise was selling so well – vast amounts – that the band/management decided to keep using him. I had actually designed several other characters to take his place but they turned out not to be needed.'

Even though Eddie's likeness would stay pretty much the same as the band quickly established their own style, Riggs told Ytsejam.com, 'I have never had a constant style. My style fluctuates from painting to painting. I can't even draw three pictures in pen and ink and have them all come out in the same style ... I am getting better as I get older but the same thing persists to some degree. I have always tended to experiment a lot, both with imagery and with materials ... not always with good results.'

Where any evolutions in Eddie's appearance were concerned, the artist told CNN that he and the band maintained something of a collaborative effort. 'The various looks of Eddie are often derived from the direction that the band wants to go in at the time. One year it was Egyptian, another year it was sci-fi and so on. Usually the details of what came after were my doing. They just gave me a direction and then let me run with it. Most of the time the rest of the content was my idea, although sometimes they would have ideas for the actual content of a painting, like the *Piece of Mind* cover, which was Steve's idea. A lot of the other stuff, the detail and such, I used to make up as I went along. Sometimes I just got bored and changed him anyway, for something to do.'

As for how the interaction with Iron Maiden worked, Riggs told *Storytelling Magazine*, 'I would get a title or the title and a direction to go in, and then I would send a sketch to the manager, Rod Smallwood. We would talk over the idea and decide if Rod felt it needed anything. Quite often he would just say go ahead and I would get on with the job. For example, the brief I got for *Somewhere in Time* was, "We want a city like the one in *Blade Runner*," and the rest was left pretty much up to me. The look of Eddie was my invention, as was the content of the city. Steve came to me near the end of the work and asked if I could include some little details.'

Regarding his own influences as an artist, Riggs shared with Ytsejam.com, 'I like Max Ernst, Joan Miro, Piet Mondrian, Kandinsky, some Picasso and some Braque. Other artists are not much of an influence on my illustration work – I tend to work from my own inner vision. Whenever I have tried to paint in other people's style, I've found it depressing and boring so I don't do it.'

Going into more detail with 89.8FM 'Solid Rock' host Andy Lee, he added, 'I used to like a bit of Savador Dali but he was never a great influence. I used to quite like comic artists, like Jack Kirby and a couple of people like that. I used to draw a lot when I was about fourteen. I didn't use to do a lot of painting – I had to teach myself to paint when I got to about eighteen. I suddenly realised you couldn't just do the drawing thing, and that you have to actually paint stuff. It took a while to dawn. I fancied being a comic artist when I was younger until I realised I couldn't bear to paint the same thing day in and day out ... then I ended up painting Eddie for twenty years.'

Elaborating on the technical details of portraying Eddie, Riggs told *Lollipop*, 'All the Iron Maiden work was done with acrylic paint on illustration board,' adding to Ytsejam.com, 'My artwork was *never* drawn – it was painted in gouache, acrylic and Alkyd [oil] paints on illustration board. I moved over to computer-based illustration because it is a better medium for producing commercial illustration. Painting with a stick is better than painting with your fingers, painting with a brush is better than using a stick [and] computer is better than using a brush. It's the only way to get the work done in the time allowed to the quality required.

'I have never painted because I like using paint – I paint because I want to make an image. It is the image that is paramount, not the painting technique. Using a computer is the best method currently available for making an image. All this is true for commercial illustration only – for other mediums you must make other choices.'

Delving deeper into his ways of working, the artist added, 'I work in bits. I render all the modes separately and put them together with bits of photography and illustration at the end. This gives me more scope to move things about but you have to be careful with the lighting – make sure it is all from the right direction. I use the following software: Bryce for rendering and some modelling; Inspire 3D for modelling mostly and some rendering; Strata 3D for modelling and rendering; Illustrator for line work; Photoshop for putting all the bits together, and also for photomontage and illustrating. Photoshop is the best for this – do not believe the hype on the boxes of the other packages. For illustrating I prefer the computer. I also paint some abstract pictures: for this I prefer paint. Oil is nice but anything will do.'

Despite the fact he was designing Maiden's album covers, Riggs revealed that their music was not an inspiration. 'I usually play the things they send to me once or twice but I find music is very distracting for me so I don't play it when I am working.' The artist added to *Lollipop*, 'When I'm doing the easy bits, I sometimes listen to music but, when I'm trying to concentrate, it gets on my nerves. It's too distracting. I tend to paint late at night and the same goes for computer art ... I tend to be rather nocturnal anyway.'

As for bringing Eddie to life on stage, Riggs told *Lollipop*, 'I painted the first Eddie backdrop – actually, the first three or four – and then I managed to get out of doing them because they were horrible to have to do. You end up getting shipped across London to some lonely, cold, wet warehouse with sheets of canvas and a bucket of paint.'

Turning to the artwork for the single 'Twilight Zone' as an example, Riggs recalled to Ytsejam.com, 'I brought some new drawing board and, when I came to put the paint on to it, it slid around like it was on greaseproof paper. I didn't have any of the good board left, and I couldn't get any more because it was

Sunday and the shops were closed. The artwork had to be finished by Monday morning so I had no choice but to patch it up with an airbrush and call it finished.'

That trend stayed the same throughout his designs for the band's next few studio LPs. 'Most of the early works were done in a single weekend,' Riggs recalled in the same conversation. 'They would phone me up on Thursday night and say, "We need it by Monday morning," so I would do it in two and a half days. This was the case right up to *The Number of the Beast* – a picture I did in two days for the single but it got used as the album cover. This ridiculous time constraint is the main reason why a lot of the figure work in those pictures is a bit rough.'

For 1986's *Somewhere in Time*, the artist told *Lollipop* of his original big-city scene, 'They wanted it to look more *Blade Runner* than *Star Wars* and, up in the sky, I had the USS *Enterprise* and a few other well-known starships. They made me take them out so they wouldn't get sued. But I stuck Batman standing on a ledge on the back sleeve. That was about three years before the Batman movie came out. And if you look at the front window of the building, there's a reflection of a street sign across the road that, if you read it backwards, says, "This is a very boring painting."

'I like to stick any old rubbish in there ... I managed to get Mickey Mouse in there one time without getting caught. It was on the single for "Twilight Zone". There's a woman sitting in front of a mirror with Eddie appearing in the reflection behind her and, behind a photo of Eddie on the dresser, Mickey Mouse is poking his head around at her.'

Unlike past album covers, where he had had to rush his work, Riggs said that, with *Somewhere in Time*, 'I worked on that for so long I started hallucinating. I had to stop for two weeks because I wasn't doing any work. I just sat in front of the painting, imagining where all these little characters were going and what their lives were like. I don't have nightmares and then paint them, as some people might think – it all starts and ends on the canvas.' Despite his travails in coming up with the finished product, the artist told *Storyteller Magazine* that this cover remained one of his favourites 'because of the detail. I like the detail ... [and] *Stranger in a Strange Land* because it looks like Clint Eastwood.'

When it came to the later 1980s Maiden albums, beginning with 1988's *Seventh Son of a Seventh Son* and the covers for its singles in particular, Riggs confessed to *Storyteller Magazine* that he loved 'The Clairvoyant' and 'Can I Play with Madness' because they are 'so ape shit'. Going into more detail with CNN, he said, 'I like "The Clairvoyant" because it's so completely manic. I didn't plan it like that. I started out with an idea for something like the Roman god Janus, who had two faces, and then I gave him three faces [past, present and future] but I couldn't reconcile his face when his mouth was open. So in desperation I rubbed out the bits between his lower and upper jaw [his cheeks] and it looked so mad that I left it like that.'

In 1990, to the shock of fans, it was announced that, after a decade of work together, Riggs and Maiden were parting company. It turned out that this was largely over disagreements over the sleeve of *Fear of the Dark*, for which Riggs had done the initial designs. Riggs recalled to Ytsejam.com, 'On this album they just kept changing their mind about everything. They would ask me for sketches about vampires so I would go away and do sketches of vampires. Then I would show them to the manager and he would say, "Why are you drawing vampires? We are into werewolves now," and I would say, "Thanks for telling me ..." And so it went: every time I did anything, they would just throw it back at me and say, "That's not what we want any more – we want this now."

'So, in the end, I just got sick of all the bullshit and stopped working. As it turns out, they were giving all the ideas to several other artists as well because they thought anyone could paint Eddie. So, when I stopped working, the only picture they had that was usable was an unfinished picture of Eddie as a tree ... which is what they used. I think the real problem was that my artwork was getting more attention than the band really liked and they thought they would see if they could use other artists instead.'

Following Riggs' departure, the band took up with Melvyn Grant, who designed the cover art for *Fear of the Dark*, *Virtual XI* and *The Final Frontier*, among others. In conversation with the UK's *The Examiner*, Grant explained how he sought to distinguish – albeit subtly – his own Eddie design from that of Riggs. 'The original Eddie seemed to be very happy causing all sorts of chaos, and hacking people to bits with axes and things like that. I did want to put more psychological tension in it.

'For instance, on *Fear of the Dark*, the first one I did, I don't think many people realise that Eddie is not actually sitting in the tree. He's actually coming down the tree. So you can really look at it either way. The body is coming down from the tree and it looks like Eddie has a tail close to the moon. I try to put a little more depth into it aside from utter brutality.'

To Grant's relief, when word came back from the band, it was positive. 'After I did the first teaser Rod Smallwood called me and said how much he really liked it. His words, I think, were, "Fucking amazing!" Which was very nice of him to do because they were very busy setting up this tour. Everything was happening all at once and yet I [found] that they are very nice people to deal with.'

Elaborating on what he felt he had captured in his rendition of Eddie to make him the band's new go-to guy, Grant explained to the Italian Iron Maiden fanzine *Eddies*, 'Sanctuary asked me to come up with ideas for an image to go with the title *Fear of the Dark*. They gave me no direction other than the title. It was a free run. So I went off and produced a few pencil drawings, of which the Tree Eddie was one. I had wanted to redesign the look of Eddie quite extensively but Sanctuary said to keep it close to the original.

'Here is a small eerie tale that you may find of interest, which happened to me while I was finishing the painting of *Fear of the Dark*. I have never told this to anyone until now. I had never experienced anything like it before and it has never happened to me since. And no, I do not take any substances.

'Towards the end of painting *Fear of the Dark*, I was

working alone in my studio. It was late at night and I was running on a high, completely absorbed in the painting – that feeling of mental overdrive, which often happens when I really get into my work. This is when I'm truly creative. All sorts of stuff jumps in and out of my head, and I really enjoy this state. It's like meditating at warp speed. But this time it was different. As the images flowed through my head some became increasingly persistent, like a strange and disturbing story. Every detail was so clear, like nothing I had ever experienced. And gradually it trapped all my senses – so vividly that, years later, I can still clearly see the imagery and hear the peculiar, wind-torn gurgle that drove it on.

'Part of the spookiness of Eddie in the *Fear of the Dark* painting is that the image is really double edged. Eddie's shoulders, head and arms, at first glance, fit the body fused to the tree in the sitting position but, if you look further, they also belong to the less obvious body coming down the trunk. The dark branch at the top edge of the moon is a kind of tail and the legs would carry on up the main trunk or maybe his upward lower body is more snake-like. This begs the question: which body is which? If Eddie is really coming down the tree and the other body is not Eddie's, then who, or what, is sitting in the tree?'

Grant joked, 'Maybe I could have shown Eddie as a cute Romeo with a cheeky twinkle in his eye. But I don't think so. Eddie would sooner axe you as look at you. And that's always been his pleasure. Any twinkle in his eye happened just as the blade fell. So my approach to *Fear of the Dark* was to see how sinister I could make Eddie. We've had all the physical violence with the blood and sharp things – now let's instil something more psychological. So I created this Eddie as part of a tree set in a pleasant wood that you might like to wander through on a beautiful moonlit night, thinking all is wonderful. But, unbeknown, the trail would lead a poor innocent soul straight to Eddie's lair and, even if you had no fear of the dark at the time, you definitely would from then on.'

Talking about his way of working as an artist, Grant added, 'At the time of painting *Fear of the Dark* and *Virtual XI* I was using oil paints on board, as I'd been doing for many years. *Death on the Road* and "The Reincarnation of Benjamin Breeg" were painted digitally. Mostly now for commercial work, I paint digitally. I use Photoshop and sometimes Painter on a G5 Desktop Pro Mac. But I don't produce anything computer generated – everything I produce I have to work at. I apply it the same as I would with oil painting, stroke upon stroke. It's just now pixel on screen instead of paint on board. It's a lot quicker and cleaner. No paint to dry but I do miss playing around with oil paint.'

Turning to the actual concepts for Maiden covers, Grant added to *The Examiner* that, typically, 'they actually have a rough idea of what they want. They know sort of what they want but they don't really know what they want. When you start doing things, that is what triggers their imaginations and that's when they want something changed.'

When he sat down to design *Virtual XI*, for example, the artist recalled to *Eddies* that 'Maiden asked for an idea to do with Virtual Reality. The concept behind *Virtual XI* (which I originally called *Virtual Insanity*) was of a boy sitting in a very tranquil setting, seeing Eddie and chaos through the VR set. So which world is the boy actually in? I was then asked to include the football game, which is how the title became *Virtual XI*.'

In channeling his muse throughout the course of designing any Eddie variation, the artist revealed, 'I'm not too sure what the "primal creative force" is exactly but it sounds good and I hope I have it by the bucketful. But I do a lot of reading and I like to watch movies. I like to dream too but not the types that wake you in a cold sweat, like nightmares that don't wear pyjamas.'

Looking to the future as the 1990s unfolded, Grant was quite candid in his conversation with *The Examiner*. 'Derek Riggs and his style of artwork never appealed to me so, naturally, I wanted to change it and do my version of Eddie. But that was stopped by Maiden, who didn't want me to stray too far from the original style, which obviously all of the band's fans like. You get so used to something that it becomes your thing and you fall in love with that version of Eddie.

'I did try to change him a bit, in a way that suited me and made me happier with it. The first two paintings I did for Iron Maiden were for *Fear of the Dark* and *Virtual XI*. They were both actually oil paintings and I dealt with Iron Maiden directly through my agent. And that was fine. Then, with *Death on the Road*, it came through a design studio and that's how it's been ever since. I think, when you're going through three or four people, that's where things get muddled and changed around. That's what takes up too much time.'

When the band's 30th anniversary rolled around in 2010, they were preparing the release of *The Final Frontier*, with Grant once again at the designing helm. In discussing his artistic process for the cover art's creation, the artist said to *The Examiner*, 'I did various sketches based on the title alone. Then they came up with the idea of doing something on the spacecraft. Originally, when I did it, it wasn't Eddie reaching in like he is – he was more meaty-like and stealthier in a more evil way. Originally, they didn't want the spacecraft all ripped to shreds. They wanted it to look like a hatch had come off and there would be a skeletal crew inside. So I wanted to make Eddie almost slither in. But, gradually, it molded into the more brutal one, which is what you see now.

'When I was showing them the several sketches of my ideas, Rod liked the head-on one of the Eddies and he asked me if I could do a front view of that head, one with the mouth closed and one with the mouth open. So I did a pencil of that, which he and the studio really liked.'

But the job wasn't done yet. 'It got passed over to Steve and Bruce [but] they weren't happy with it because it wasn't gruesome enough. Steve didn't say much but Bruce gave a lot of comments on it. So then I did one with half the head putrefied and diseased while the other half was OK, sent them over, and they really liked that. That then became the teaser poster.'

Still, the delays, Grant felt, were in the best interest of the final product. 'You try it one way and they go, "Can we change this?" or, "Can we move this around slightly?" So the whole thing is repainted time and time again ... They always want to give their fans something fresh; something new.'

Reflecting on his contribution to the creative evolution of Eddie's 30 years as Iron Maiden's flagship mascot and merchandising money machine, Grant told *Eddies*, 'Eddie is a very important visual part of the whole Iron Maiden experience. Just show Eddie and people think of Maiden. He's like the final member of the band. He's the real crazy one waiting just out of sight that scouts ahead and, of course, being Eddie and unaccountable, he can do anything he likes. I think Eddie has helped give Iron Maiden a top universal image.'

When asked about his own part in sustaining and expanding this visual staple of Maiden's image, Grant's answer was, 'It's difficult for me to know whether or not my artworks are key points. I do the paintings, within the limitations of the brief, as best I can at the time and have as much fun as I can in doing them. The feedback that has filtered back to me has been good so that pleases me ... My aim in creating images is to give something unique that I see, hopefully something of benefit, a communication to the viewer.'

In his own reflections on how the phenomenon of Eddie made him a 'cult icon', original artist Derek Riggs told Ytsejam.com, 'I just sit here and paint pictures for anyone who pays me. The cult-icon thing really doesn't affect my life in any way at all. It's not as if I get recognised in the street or anything and I am not personally famous in any way ... just people like my pictures sometimes.'

CONCLUSION

2011 AND BEYOND . . .

'If you don't like Iron Maiden, to me you are not much of a metalhead'
Metal-Rules.com

'In the loud and fast genre of heavy metal, Iron Maiden's music is tough to beat'
The National Review

'We always like to do our own thing and not think about what's going on around us'
Steve Harris

As metal bands go, Iron Maiden is the equivalent of a 1978 Corvette Coupe, still motoring along as popular as ever. The second decade of the new Millennium celebrates them as a living legend, as the band continues to crank out platinum album after album in the studio and play before multiple generations of fans – they were one of the top touring acts of 2010 with more than $12 million in US grosses alone.

As *Spin* magazine noted in 2010 of the band's continued vitality, 'It's easy to forget, amid the constant deluge of news about the cratering music industry, that a few lucky bands are thriving, seemingly oblivious to the realities of their peers and contemporaries. Long-running UK metal heroes Iron Maiden have to top that list. Iron Maiden have already proven themselves recession proof and even death-of-the-music-industry proof.'

Celebrating the band's longevity and legacy, *Stylus* magazine pointed out that 'the band could have succumbed to the nostalgia circuit like so many of its contemporaries. However, the mighty Maiden is not only still productive but also influential.' *Brave Words/Bloody Knuckles* magazine echoed that 'Iron Maiden continue to inspire debate because what they do matters to the metal community as a whole'.

A key part of the band's strategy for staying on the cutting edge of heavy metal, according to the BBC, begins with the fact that 'Maiden don't really do playing it safe.' As a result, it adds, 'Beginning with front man Bruce Dickinson's return to the band in 1999, Maiden have embarked on the most successful phase of their career whilst fully indulging their progressive tendencies.'

On one hand, as the *LA Times* noted, 'Maiden has retained certain sonic signatures: Thin Lizzy/Wishbone Ash-inspired twin-axe harmonising; ominous Black Sabbath-y riffs; a prog-lite sense of structural adventure; Harris's clanking basslines; and flecks of folk-rock.' On the other hand, as the band's label, EMI, enthused, 'Thirty years after their debut album in April 1980 and with more than 80 million albums sold, Iron Maiden are more creatively vibrant, dynamic and relevant than ever, reaching a new pinnacle in their career and still adding legions of new young fans to their ever-increasing following.'

Iron Maiden's reign over heavy metal only promises to grow with the band's announcement they were teaming with the wildly popular *Rock Star* video-game series. Its Senior Vice President, Paul DeGooyer, underscored just how in demand the band were when he said to the press, 'Metal fans have wanted this one for a long time and we've answered them with some of the greatest Maiden songs, both live and recorded. Iron Maiden is one of the most successful and widely recognised metal bands of all time.'

For the band's members, according to band bassist, founder and chief songwriter Steve Harris, the No. 1 focus remains squarely on continuing to produce new music that 'keeps things fresh for us and the fans'. As he added in his closing promise to NME, 'The band has had a really long career and who knows when it's gonna stop? We don't feel like we're there yet ...'